Praise for Michael Okon

"… *brings his buoyant mix of terror and humor to a tale of three major monsters of classic horror … his take on zombies, werewolves, and vampires is rooted in warmly likeably characters … the adventure ramps up to an enjoyably gore-soaked finale … full of both mayhem and heart.*"

—*Kirkus Review*

"… *toys with our preconceptions of scary creatures in his delightfully entertaining novel … part satire, part coming-of-age story, part genre gore-fest,* Monsterland *is smart, campy fun … peppers the narrative with real-life significance … a talented and clever enough writer to imbue his characters with real emotion … it is this deepening of the plot that elevates* Monsterland *above standard monster fare … the novel will prove an entertaining and thought-provoking read for both teenagers and adults.*"

—Scott Neuffer, *Foreword Reviews*

MICHAEL OKON

MONSTERLAND

WORDFIRE PRESS
COLORADO SPRINGS, COLORADO

ISBN: 978-1-61475-594-4

Cover painting by Michael Mastermaker

Cover design by Michael Mastermaker

Edited by Kevin J. Anderson

Kevin J. Anderson, Art Director

Published by WordFire Press, an imprint of WordFire, LLC PO Box 1840 Monument CO 80132

Kevin J. Anderson & Rebecca Moesta, Publishers

WordFire Press Trade Paperback Edition October 2017 Printed in the USA wordfirepress.com

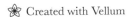 Created with Vellum

Dedication

For Eric, my monster movie companion.

To Sharon, Alexander, Cayla, Jennifer, Hallie, Zachary, Mom, and Dad,

To Susan, Nick, Kim, Brittney, Julie, Dave, Kevin, and WordFire Press ...

A friend is someone who will bail you out of jail. A best friend is the one sitting next to you saying, "boy that was fun." - The Maugles

Thank you all for being my best friends.

Courage is being scared to death ... and saddling up anyway.

John Wayne

Chapter 1

The Everglades

The fire Billy created burned bright; rabbits roasted on a spit made from hickory, the juices dripping to hiss in the flames. Seven of his hairy friends lay in scattered repose, enjoying the late afternoon lull—two napped, the others tossed a stuffed fur in the form of a ball around the clearing, hooting with amusement when it rolled into the brush. They traveled in a pack, his group, his makeshift family, foraging together, hiding in plain sight. It had been that way for generations. But the glades were getting smaller, the humans invasive.

Mosquitoes droned lazily over the still water. Frogs croaked while they sunbathed on waxy lily pads. The sun started its slow descent to the horizon, hot pink and lilac clouds rippling against the empty canvas of the sky. Here and there, fireflies lit the gloom, doing a placid ballet in the humid air.

Unseen, the men moved closer to the campfire as the sun sank into the western treetops.

A lone hawk cried out a warning, disturbing the peace of

the glade. Huge birds answered, flapping their wings, creating a cacophony of swamp sounds. The area became a concerto of animals responding to the disruption of their home—wild screams, squeaks, and complaints of the invasion of their territory.

Billy stood, his head tilted as he listened intently. He heard a melody, that strange organization of sounds, predictable as well as dangerous. It had been years since he'd heard music. His stomach clenched with uneasiness. Where those rhythms originated meant only one thing—they were not alone in the swamp.

His pack rose, tense and alert, their eyes watching the waterway. Billy silently parted the thick leaves to expose a flat-bottom boat with dangerous strangers floating slowly toward them.

The boat was filled with people, excitedly searching the banks of the swamp, their expensive khaki bush clothes ringed with sweat.

Little John, Billy's best friend, leaned closer and whispered, "Tourists?"

Billy noticed the rifles before the rest of the group. He held up his hand signaling for silence. "Not tourists. Enemies," he replied.

Men's voices drifted on the turgid air.

This is no good, Billy thought furiously. He was gauging the time, his eyes opening wide. It was late. They had to get out of there. *It's going to happen, and those people are going to see it.*

The bald top of the moon peeked over the line of trees in the south, the sky graying to twilight with each passing second. Night came fast in the swamp, dropping a curtain of darkness, extinguishing all light except for the beacon of the full moon. It continued to float upward, indifferent to the consequences for its innocent victims.

A halo of lighter blue surrounded the globe, limning the

trees silver, the cobwebs in the branches becoming chains of dripping diamonds in the coming night.

What do these strangers want? Billy fought the urge to scream. *This is our home. Humans don't belong in the swamp.*

The moon continued to rise, the familiar agony beginning in his chest. A full moon, a dangerous moon. Billy fought the demons churning within his body, feeling the pain of metamorphosis.

He curled inward, hunching his shoulders, the curse of his nature making his spine pull until his tendons and muscles tore from their human positions to transform into something wicked.

A howl erupted from his throat, followed by another, and then another. Grabbing handfuls of dirt, he tried to fight the awful change, but, as the sun set, the moon took control of his life, and the unnatural force tore through his unwilling body.

Reason fled, his heart raced. Falling on his hands and knees, Billy let loose a keening cry as his face elongated, his body changing into a canine, fangs filling his mouth. He raced in a circle in a demented dance, knowing his fellow pack members did the same thing.

Slowing, he regulated his labored breathing, forcing the icy calmness he needed to keep some semblance of reason. He peered through the dense brush. Lights from the search party bobbed in between the thick reeds. The odor, the stench of humanity, filled the clearing. The enemy had arrived.

He turned, digging furiously on the ground, throwing dirt on the campfire flames, hiding their existence. Discovery would ruin everything. No one could live with their kind.

Humans brought disease; humans brought anger; humans brought hatred. They were there; he could smell them, see their clumsy bodies splashing through the bog.

"They've found us," he growled in the unique language they used after transformation. "Run!" he barked as he turned to his pack, watching his friends' naked skin transform until it was covered with the same silvered fur.

They cried out in unison at the pain, howling with the injustice, and then ran in fear from the interlopers threatening their habitat.

They separated into two groups and took off in different directions to confuse the strangers.

Billy tore through the brush, thorns ripping his fur, and, in his adrenaline rush, he didn't feel anything. He glanced backward; the humans were chasing them, one running with a huge camera. Nine other hunters followed, the long barrels of their rifles bearing down on them.

Behind him, he heard multiple shots and triumphant shouts, knowing that his friends were succumbing one by one.

With a frantic growl, he urged Little John, Petey, and Todd to run faster.

Little John's massive body was blocking him. Billy bayed at him to keep his head closer to the ground. He worried about Little John, knowing that his big frame might as well have had a target painted on it.

"Stay close together," he urged. His heart sank when he heard Todd yelp. The shot hit his friend from behind, sending him careening into a trench. Billy wanted to stop but knew he couldn't help Todd. The humans were on his friend's fallen body seconds later. He had to find Petey and Little John a place to hide.

There was a loud scream as one of their pursuers stumbled on a root to their left. Billy paused, panting wildly, to get his bearings next to the broad trunk of a cypress tree.

"Which way?" Petey asked.

Billy's eyes searched the tangle of the mangroves for an opening.

A shot rang out, splintering a tree, sending shards of bark around them. Billy reared in surprised shock. It wasn't a bullet. A red feathered dart was vibrating next to him, sticking out of the wood.

"What is that?" Petey whimpered.

"It's a dart," Billy said. "They're trying to capture us. This way!"

He and his packmates took off, disappearing into the twisted vines.

They clawed through the swamp, hiding behind clusters of Spanish moss, dipping under the water when the hunters approached.

One man in the group stood taller and leaner than the rest, his dark wolfish eyes scanning the dense undergrowth looking for them. The man paused, training his gun in Billy's direction as if he could see straight through the foliage.

Billy held his breath, terrified of discovery, but the harried sounds of a chase distracted the leader of the hunters.

Billy and his pack skirted solid ground, their bodies quivering. He glanced at the sky, wishing for the sun to rise so that he would transform back to being human.

The splashes of their pursuers seemed to recede. The pack waited in claustrophobic silence for the time to pass.

Billy spied a dinghy heading towards the flat-bottom boat as dawn approached. They heard the sputter of an engine being turned over.

"They're leaving," Little John said hopefully.

The rays of the sun lit the eastern sky. It was quiet once more. They paddled softly toward the shore. Coming out of the water, they shook themselves of the muck. Early morning birdcalls broke out in the thick stillness.

Billy barked a cry of dismay as shots rang out. Little John went down in a tumble of leaves and mud, a dart silencing him.

Billy veered right, squirming under a broken log, Petey barreling over it. The report of another shot and a loud thump told him that he had lost Petey too.

What do they want from us?

Billy dug his paws into the marshy land, his heart pumping like a piston. He leaped high over an alligator dozing in the shade of a leafy tree. Billy felt the impact of a dart, a sharp pain ripping into his flank.

His eyes dimmed as he tumbled headlong onto the boggy ground. He rolled over and over, coming to rest on a bed of rotting leaves. He couldn't move; his limbs were leaden. His ears registered the sound of running feet.

Billy looked up into the triumphant, black eyes of the man who led the attack. The hunter placed his boot on his neck, holding him down.

"Got ya," he heard the man say with a thick accent before everything went dark.

Chapter 2

Copper Valley—the Badlands in California

The house was little more than a bungalow with a screened porch that doubled as a den in the summer. Carter White had his feet on a ratty old ottoman, his large frame sprawled on the flowered couch he'd inherited from his aunt Junie when she died. They had blended all their furniture when they married, Gracie and him. Admittedly, it wasn't much, but with her two monsters, it didn't pay to have new furnishings.

Maybe "monsters" was a tad too extreme, Carter admitted. Sean was a handful, but Wyatt was a good kid. They were Gracie's sons—Sean was fourteen, and Wyatt was turning eighteen this spring, right before graduation, which was five weeks away.

He and Gracie had been together for two years, meeting a year after her divorce when she moved back to Copper Valley and into her folks' old place. They finally tied the knot early this past September, and six months later they got word that Gracie's ex, Frank, had died suddenly while on a job.

Sean burst through the screen door, practically ripping it off its hinges.

"Hey!" Carter shouted in his best highway patrol voice. "Take it easy."

Sean paused, breathing hard, his feet encased in the red mud of the high desert, his tennis shoes stained as if he had just left a crime scene.

"Your mom's gonna kill you." Carter looked down at his stepson's feet. "Don't track that stuff in here."

Sean threw his knapsack on the faded couch and then ripped off his shirt to wipe down the white leather of his sneakers. "Dammit," he muttered.

"Hey, now." Carter lowered the sound on the television, his news program forgotten. He gave the youngster an arch look. "You running in the wash again?" The wash was a gully that ran parallel to the school. Gracie was too lenient, and he was in that cloudy area when it came to parenting. He found his disciplining methods meeting head on with the "you're not my father" comment.

They were still working on his role in the kids' lives. While they seemed to like him well enough, hit the hoops and watched baseball with him, they kindly rejected his offer to call him *Dad*, and, more often than not, he was made to feel unwelcome in their tight trio. He put that down to their closeness after the abusive relationship they'd had with their father.

Frank Baldwin was a creep, a lying, low-down, crooked lawyer who liked to torment Gracie and make the kids choose sides. He pushed them away with his selfish ambition, cloaked in concern for the well-being of his family. Frank had left them high and dry, with Carter's cop salary and Gracie's teaching job supporting them. Frank donated all his money to some hole-in-the-wall charity. *Well, none of that mattered now,* Carter thought. He had it under control. Still, when Frank crooked his finger, the kids ran to see him. But now he was gone, and somehow it ruined the peace of their home. Carter couldn't put his finger on it, but he knew it was true.

"Nah ... um, no. I—" Sean's reply was cut off by pounding footsteps. Sean spun quickly, latching the flimsy screen door, and then burst out laughing. Wyatt slammed his fist against the chipped green paint of the door.

"Sean!" he shouted, his eyes narrowed with anger. "Sean, I'm gonna kill you."

Carter unfolded himself from his comfortable spot, his six-foot-four-inch body filling the crowded room. "Did some damage, Sean?" he asked quietly.

Sean shrugged indifferently, bolting when Carter motioned for him to leave with a slight nod.

Carter unlatched and then caught the abused screen door as Wyatt yanked it open. "Hard day?"

"Where is he? I'm gonna rip the little bastard apart." Wyatt drew his breath in great gulping sobs. A crumpled piece of paper was fisted in his hand.

"I have it on the best authority that your parents were well and truly married when Sean entered this world. Little brothers are the devil. Sit down and cool off."

Wyatt pushed forward, but the large, warm hand on his shoulder slowed him down. He saw Carter's gentle gray eyes look pointedly at the sofa, his eyebrows raised in silent question. Wyatt ungraciously threw himself onto the sagging pillows, releasing a cloud of ever-present dust.

They sat in silence, Carter relaxing back in his spot, the television droning in the background. Carter watched his stepson struggle to calm himself. It was evident he was livid, filled with fury. He saw Wyatt squeeze the piece of paper in his hand into a tight ball, crushing it. Wyatt's foot jiggled with impatience. He had tried hard to find common ground, but, other than basketball and the new theme park, Carter had few interests to connect with the kids.

He tried to take him shooting in the desert, but Wyatt

called it a mindless activity, and that was the end of that. Wyatt had a problem with the loudness of the guns. Carter would watch his stepson flinch with each shot fired.

The noise never bothered Sean, the more rascally of the two. He knew that while Sean loved the loud report of the guns, Wyatt seemed afraid of the noise. They lived in careful respect; he was aware that Wyatt was heartily disappointed that he was not going away to college in the fall. They were cramped in the old house, but it was the best they could do under the circumstances.

Frank left them no estate, even though Gracie was sure he had buckets of money. The lawyer said it was gone, eaten up by their costly divorce, and the balance given to charity. No way to treat a family, in Carter's opinion. Hell, he gave up his bike to help get Wyatt his first car. It was a jalopy, but it had four wheels and a gas tank.

Carter eyed him from his spot, deftly changing the subject to baseball. They discussed last night's Sidewinders game; Wyatt lost his sullenness. *The kid had a great batting arm,* Carter thought proudly. He wished he'd do something with it, other than the occasional sandlot game.

He pointed the remote to the old hospital-issued television bolted to the corner of the room. They had bought it at an auction when County General closed last year. They were forced to travel thirty miles for medical help until Vincent Konrad gifted the small community with a huge medical center for allowing the building of his new theme park. The new hospital was opening now, bigger and better than the one the city shut down due to budget cuts. It was creating a lot of jobs, and the theme park would be bringing in a boatload of tourists, which, in turn, infused necessary cash into the starving town.

The goddamned water had been turned off six months ago. If not for Saint Vincent buying them the rights to the San

Simi pipeline, they would have pretty much had to abandon their homes.

Copper Valley was out of money, as were most small towns and even some of the larger cities in America. The police force, fire department, and paramedics were on the verge of being shut down, city hall right behind them. The vagrant population, jobless people who traveled from town to town looking for work, had tripled, bringing crime to the bucolic streets of the sleepy enclave.

Vincent's business plan provided both housing and employment, enabling the homeless to get off the village streets. While there had been no outbreak of the virus in California, the entire country's economy suffered as the world dealt with the pandemic that had broken out two years ago.

The virus started in East Asia, but quick thinking from the World Health Organization isolated it with containment camps. They'd had plenty of practice with the Ebola outbreaks of the last decade.

Carter shivered, thinking of those poor souls who caught the disease. There had been a few cases in the States, mostly doctors and aid workers who brought it home after going to help the victims. It spread, but the government was quick to create two big settlements to keep the infected away from the population, much like the leper colonies from ancient times. It killed the economy though. People were afraid to travel or accept goods from overseas.

Even with all that, Carter couldn't believe what was happening to his home. The city council practically prostrated themselves with gratitude when Vincent picked the sleepy town as the spot for his park. The government even green-lit the macabre idea.

It was creepy, using victims of the plague as a tourist attraction, and it reminded him of that ghoulish exhibit called *Bodies* where they embalmed dead people's remains in plastic so people could see how humans worked.

Carter's lips tightened. Saint Vincent seemed too good to be true. He swooped in and bargained for a fresh water supply, built the fancy medical center, repaved the gutted roads, breathing life back into the dying community. Everybody loved him, except for Carter White. He watched Wyatt's anger drain to be replaced by an interest in the show. Wyatt thought Vincent walked on water.

"Ah …," Carter said looking back at the television set. "Your hero." He turned the sound up. Vincent Konrad was being interviewed on the news.

Wyatt expertly tossed the crumpled paper into a metal trash can decorated with the vintage video game characters from his youth. It was a recent reject from his room. He didn't want it up there anymore. He had thrown out most of the junk he'd taken with him from Los Angeles—kid's stuff, action figures, his werewolf head pendant. He had other interests now.

Carter nodded with appreciation. "Nothing but net."

Wyatt shrugged, his face downcast. "Why don't you like Vincent Konrad? At least he's trying to do something to help get this country out of its depression."

Carter studied Vincent's face on the set without answering. The doctor could be anywhere from fifty to eighty. His dun-colored hair was combed straight back from his high, white forehead. He had deep-set dark eyes, a long, thin nose, and a slash of a mouth. His narrow face looked right at the camera without any trace of warmth or humor.

Carter considered his stepson's serious face and said, "The answer is not camouflaging the problems and making a game out of it."

"It's a solution. I don't see anything else working."

That was true. Carter frowned. Washington was dead-locked on whether these new species had rights and should be treated equally to other citizens. Either way, the world had changed drastically and wasn't prepared to handle the new developments.

There was trouble everywhere. The world economy was being held together with duct tape. The only thing world leaders seemed to agree on was Dr. Vincent Konrad. Vincent Konrad appeared out of nowhere with a plan, and all the governments grabbed his idea with eager hands.

Carter turned back to the television. He wasn't in the mood to argue with Wyatt about it anymore. Wyatt was smart, had gone to the best schools in Los Angeles when his parents were together. If not for the divorce, he'd probably be headed for an Ivy League school this fall.

Carter knew Wyatt had a hard time fitting in this dumpy, little town. It was a close-knit community that didn't particularly welcome newcomers, but Gracie landed a teaching job here, and they had relocated. He admired Wyatt for never complaining. The kid had made the best of it, finding friends with a fringe group, the ones that were just a little off. He wished the boy wouldn't back off so quickly but wasn't quite sure how to teach him to stand up for himself.

Carter had never had kids, and becoming a father to two nearly grown boys wasn't so easy for him either. *It wasn't like there was a handbook on this stuff,* he thought, turning his attention back to the television.

The program was a weekly magazine show on a major network. Vincent Konrad was sitting opposite Joe Myers, the principal anchor of the national evening news and the host of the program. Joe Myers had a halo of white hair, with a chiseled, tan visage. His shoulders were as broad as his career. He was the captain of his ship, commanding the newsroom with the same courage and bravery as a warship. Integrity dripped from him.

"That was some offering on Wall Street today. You made history, opening at $526 per share, and closing with the bell up $83 from there."

Dr. Vincent Konrad inclined his head. He was thin to the point of emaciation, his skin so pale, he appeared a sallow yellow.

Joe Myers continued. "You came to this country with two hundred dollars in your pocket."

"Two hundred dollars, and a pocketful of dreams," Vincent said with a slick smile. His voice reflected his Moldavian roots, the tiny country sandwiched in the Carpathian Mountains, where it was reported he was descended from royalty.

"Yet you transformed that into one of the largest fortunes in the world."

"I am blessed," Vincent said calmly with his Eastern European accent.

"Care to elaborate, Dr. Konrad?"

"Only in America can a poor, homeless boy find employment and work his way up the ladder of success."

"A homeless boy with a Ph.D. in chemical engineering, as well as a medical degree." Joe smiled, revealing a mouthful of white teeth.

"I had to retake my boards and start completely over when I got to America, from the ground up."

Wyatt turned to watch his stepfather's frown. "He's the American dream."

Carter made a face but didn't reply. They turned back to the program.

"Come now, Dr. Konrad, you've personified the American dream," the newscaster said.

Wyatt nodded in both agreement and satisfaction.

"I've merely taken the beautiful opportunities laid at my feet and worked them to my best advantage." Vincent looked thoughtful, and then his ego took over. "Not many could do what I have done. I am relentless when I desire something. My natural gas facilities have afforded me the pursuit of my real dream, that of medical breakthroughs in the field of communicable diseases."

"So, from communicable diseases, explain to me the leap to your theme park, which is more of an American nightmare than an American dream."

Vincent smiled. "Just so." He crossed his long, skinny legs, resting his thin wrist on the knob of his bony knee. "The park was a solution to the problem that came from the deep steppes of Asia. As you know, the cataclysmic explosion in central Asia released a toxic gas that began the pandemic."

Myers faced the camera. "We still can't explain the catastrophe that sent a shock wave that scorched the earth throughout Asia, flattening buildings and forests for hundreds of miles. The seismic wave was picked up all the way in Washington, D.C."

Vincent smiled. "Some say it was extraterrestrials. A sonic boom, perhaps?"

Myers reflected, "It mimicked the explosion of June 1908, when something exploded high above the atmosphere over Siberia with the same strength as one thousand atomic bombs. It destroyed the tundra. Most scientists agree it was a fragment of a comet."

Vincent shook his head. "However, no virus was recorded after that explosion, contrary to the one three years ago. Last year, the combined world governments asked all the key corporations to work on solutions to containing the ... the problem."

"You are, of course, referring to the victims who caught the virus. Everybody knows that the virus first appeared two years ago. It infected pockets of the population, spreading worldwide within four weeks, creating a pandemic that was brought under control through containment. They had isolated the victims in sectioned off campuses in the wilderness until you decided to enclose them in your theme parks. Why use plague victims?"

Vincent grinned, revealing a mouthful of yellowed teeth. "I prefer to call them zombies."

"We don't like to refer to them that way. The politically correct term is *vitality-challenged*."

"You can call them anything you like," Vincent said with a leer. "I like to call those flesh-eating catatonic creatures *zombies*."

"That sounds a bit extreme." Joe shook his head.

Vincent leaned forward, his face intense. Monsters were a subject he was passionate about—he spoke urgently, as if proving his point, and his voice rose. "The disease is responsible, not I. Once their minds are infected, they can no longer control the primal urge to eat. Their single-minded determination and lack of coherency make it impossible for them to be at large with the general population. They are a danger to themselves as well as everyone else. What would you have the government do? Kill them?"

"Of course not," Myers said, placating him. "Keeping them isolated has kept the spread of the disease under control. Don't you think it's a risky exposure?"

"Nonsense. No one enters my zombie suburb without protective gear. My labs are working on a cure, dear man." Vincent inclined his saturnine head graciously. "I intend to see the eradication of the virus within five years."

"That is if it doesn't spread. You'll lose a great portion of your theme park, Dr. Konrad."

"I think we have enough to keep people entertained. With my discovery of werewolves in the Everglades—"

"That was a big story," Joe said. "Broken by KNAB news, our own Hector Milpas first reported that story two years ago."

"I was searching for Bigfoot. I do enjoy oddities." He laughed. "I produced a documentary, and, while we were shooting, the film crew happened upon a huge colony of werewolves. It seems they had been there forever."

"An amazing discovery. It earned you the Darwin Discovery Prize."

"Exactly!" Vincent clapped his hands, sitting up straight. "What an honor."

"And the vampires?"

"Everybody knows the vamps have been around us for years," Vincent sniffed. "It was natural to enclose them in a theme park to keep them safe. They are virtually extinct."

"Why not let them just die out? I mean, how many are there left?" Joe raised a white eyebrow in disbelief.

"Eighty-six or so, that we know of, and they are all living in my theme parks. We can't let them disappear."

"Sounds like you have a mission."

Vincent nodded gravely. "We have a duty to keep them safe."

"Why?" Joe asked.

"To study, of course. So we understand what makes them crave blood."

Joe sighed. "I think, Doctor, that you invite risk by perpetuating their unholy lifestyle."

"Your government has enlisted my help."

"I thought you had been naturalized a U.S. citizen."

"I am a citizen of the world. I intend to grab the problems deviling our times ...," he made a fist, his face a snarl, "and squeeze them into submission. With answers, of course," he added.

"So simple, yet so profound."

"I know!" Vincent agreed.

"It does feel a bit like exploitation." Joe was troubled.

Vincent held up his hand, using his fingers to make a point. "Number one, the creatures are contained. Number two, I've created a use for their skills; they were languishing in those prisons."

"Containment camps," Joe insisted.

"They were prisons, and these people—"

"People?" Joe said shocked.

"So then, Joe," Vincent said, "define people. What makes a human, human?"

Joe sat back in silence, studying his notes, dumbfounded.

"These *people* are being punished for being different. It's morally wrong to kill them. They are victims, not villains. They do what they are driven to do to survive, nothing more. There is no diabolical plan. They exist, we exist—we must learn to live together. We need to unite the world and come up with simple answers that will deal with these social issues in the same way. What we do in this country must be uniform with every other nation on earth. We need conformity to keep the world safe. In my parks, they are taken care of, and, more importantly, they are safe and happy."

"Safe?"

"Yes, safe from us. We are just as much a plague to them as they are to us."

Joe Myers leaned closer, his face set. "But is it safe for us?"

Vincent sat back, his face beaming. "Of course. I have everything under control, regulated."

"Nothing is foolproof."

"Let me assure you, Joe," Vincent laughed condescendingly. "I have put together an excellent team not only to run my parks but to control the inhabitants. Monsterland will be a gateway to the future for many different world issues, leading the way to solutions."

"Those are mighty big aspirations," Joe muttered.

The room went silent, Vincent's eyes blazed with an inner fire, his lips thinned, and he replied softly, "I think I am up to the task."

"Seven parks on six continents, all opening on the same day. Those are some big shoes."

"We cannot be selfish here. China, Australia, Brazil, France, South Africa, and Egypt have agreed to host the parks. The plague is a world problem, and we are determined to band together to overcome its insidious encroachment. While werewolves are indigenous to North America, the last of the vampires can be found in all countries. The problems they bring affect us all globally. Monsterland will save the planet, and Copper Valley is ground zero in the States for the parks. How we handle the different species will determine how the world moves forward in the coming decades."

"All right, then." Joe sighed. "If you could sum up your parks in one statement, what would you say?"

The camera centered on Vincent's face. He took a deep breath, looked straight into the lens, and stated, "Monsterland is dedicated to the nightmares that have created this world. They have kept us frozen in fear and unable to move forward as a society. Only when we are no longer afraid do we truly begin to live."

"I can't take it anymore," Carter said in disgust as he turned off the TV. "That guy's a parasite."

"What are you talking about?" Wyatt demanded. "The nation had just about shut down. He single-handedly revitalized the country. Monsterland will reignite the economy. It will save the world."

"Yeah, he's a real humanitarian," Carter said.

"What do you have against Monsterland?" Wyatt asked.

Carter didn't answer him; he ruffled Wyatt's head affectionately. Wyatt pulled away.

"Never mind that. Let's talk about something really important. What happened with Sean?"

Wyatt struggled for a moment and then began. "Yeah, Sean. He's the monster."

"Werewolf, vampire, or zombie?"

"Ah," Wyatt acknowledged, looking at Carter to see if he was mocking him. Satisfied that Carter was indeed interested, he continued, "The age-old question of monster superiority. Is he indestructible like a werewolf?" Wyatt stood, warming to his subject. "Or perhaps cunning as a vampire? No … he may have the coveted single-mindedness of a zombie——"

"Can't," Carter interrupted. "Minds are shot. Zombies got nothing up there."

"So you think. I have a theory about that, but my little brother may be lacking intelligence altogether. No, Sean is a garden-variety monster. No imagination, no style, no——"

"Enough. Skip the narrative." Carter held up a hand. "Just tell me what he did."

"Forget about it, Carter." Wyatt brushed him off.

Carter touched his arm. "No. What'd he do? Maybe I can help." Wyatt looked at him skeptically. Carter raised his eyebrows. "You never know until you try."

Wyatt sighed and then sat down again, his voice low. "He came up to me as we were leaving school. I was talking to Jade. You know——"

"Jade, Princess of the Dairy Queen."

Wyatt nodded and smiled at the image of Jade dressed like a princess, dispensing frozen shakes that could be served upside down.

"The cute girl with long, dark hair?"

"Yeah."

"So?"

"He slapped my back. I didn't think anything of it." Wyatt reached into the trash can, removing the crumpled ball of paper. He flattened it out. The word *desperate* was written in bold magic marker.

"You had this on your back when you spoke to her?"

Wyatt nodded glumly. Wyatt was a sweet kid, but painfully shy. Carter knew Wyatt was smitten with the elusive Jade; he couldn't figure out why. She was pretty enough but was dating the school quarterback and resident bully, which in Carter's mind didn't speak well for her character.

Carter didn't like Nolan Steward. His father owned the

car dealership downtown and was known for his aggressiveness as well.

Wyatt, on the other hand, had fallen in with the group that other kids rejected. *Nice kids,* Carter thought, *just a bit on the weird side.* Well, except for Wyatt. Now that he was turning eighteen, he seemed more settled, a little less geeky.

"She saw?"

"Everybody saw it."

"Shall I hold him down while you pummel him?" Carter threw the remote on the couch. He had taught Wyatt how to deliver a punishing noogie. He held up a hand, showing his whole fist with the knuckle of his middle finger slightly protruding.

Wyatt smiled in shared amusement. He shook his head. "Nah, he's just a kid. I save those for the bullies."

Carter wrapped his arm around Wyatt's shoulders affectionately. They were having a moment, and, for a second, Carter felt close to him. Wyatt smiled tentatively up at him. "Let's get dinner up before your mom comes home." He still topped his stepson by a few inches, but Wyatt would catch up. "Wait a sec."

Carter turned around, opening the screen door to peer into the growing dusk. The air had become strangely muggy. In the distance, he heard the wolves start their howling. While the park was five miles outside of town, the wind carried the cries. He shivered involuntarily and then latched the door. Reaching under the couch, he removed his revolver where he had hidden it, holding it loosely in the palm of his hand.

Chapter 3

West Hollywood, LA

"The way I see it, we got no choice." Raoul slid down onto the floor of the rat-infested apartment, running a hand through his long black hair.

"We never had a choice," Sylvie responded. She pulled a tattered cardigan over her white shoulders.

"Cold?" He helped her slide her arm through the sleeve.

"I'm always cold." She shivered, her purple lips pursed.

"I'm sorry." Raoul shrugged. He leaned over to kiss her mouth. He nipped her gently, drawing only a little blood. Sylvie reached over, smearing the red droplets with her thumb suggestively over his lips. His fang pierced her forefinger, impaling it.

"Ow." She pulled it away, but he captured her hand, taking her finger in his mouth, sucking on the sluggish puncture.

"Pig. Leave some for me." She pulled away.

"Look at us!" Raoul stood and parted the dusty blinds to gaze at Sunset Boulevard. He made a disgusted noise, and

Sylvie rose to peer out the window, spotting a has-been reality star running down the strip, the paparazzi in tow, his rear end exposed to the honking traffic.

"I don't want that to be us," said Sylvie.

Raoul took her hand, caressing the puncture mark on her finger. "We're practically cannibals. I almost drained you of every drop of blood last month."

Sylvie nodded, her pink hair a matted mess. She examined her pale hand, the nails nearly blue. She was as starved as her lover. She looked at Raoul. It was all his fault. He had turned her into this. It was true she had demanded it, lusted after him for months, even though he tried to avoid the outcome. He had warned her it was not a great life. Sylvie didn't care.

Back then, the lure of the stage, the road trips, the music had made her frantic to be included. For a time, they had nightly gigs, but she barely remembered them between the bloodlust and drugs. They were careful. It was dangerous to turn someone into a full vampire—the punishment: isolation in a camp in Antarctica where the cold eventually wore them out, and they died of exhaustion. Or loneliness—vamps were social, loved a celebration, a crowd. They defined party animals of the freewheeling eighties.

When they stopped recruiting, a euphemism for having sex, they simply started thinning out. Humans only became vampires by having a sexual encounter with one. Diseased blood, sickness, skin cancer, and a host of unglamorous reasons were steadily reducing the vampire population.

Fools who called themselves vampire hunters annihilated the Eastern European community. Overzealous religious fanatics wiped out the rest. It wasn't safe for them anymore, and they had nowhere to turn.

They were careful in their hunger for blood. Vampires were watchful not to leave a traceable trail. Raoul taught her well. They drank only from the homeless, or the roadies who followed them, begging to be included, so they made them into drones. They created armies of these drones, people they fed on, taking just enough blood to sate the demands of their bodies.

The drones became their slaves, doing their bidding without question. Drones never became vampires, they were simply a source for their addiction. Once the vamps stopped feeding off them, within weeks the drones reverted to their regular, boring selves.

Occasionally, the vampires went all the way, initiating another poor soul into their number, but eventually, the music died. The whole thing turned stale. Numbers dwindled. Their act got old, and the new generation laughed at them. The songs seemed silly, the music out of sync with the times. They lost their appeal. They were ridiculed. Where before they had ruled the night, had been sought after, controlled the club scene, they were now seen as tired, campy, too old to imitate. Their music and their fashion were reviled. Rejected from the venues they once ruled, they were forced onto the streets.

Oh, there was talk of a reality show a few years ago, but somehow they couldn't garner enough interest. Being a vampire was *de trop*. They were reduced to panhandling, which only brought them in contact with other vampires who were down on their luck and running from the law as well. There were just a few of their kind now. They were almost gone.

Broke, dejected, and blood-starved, they scurried from town to town, searching for their next fix of blood, hiding in the shadows.

Raoul slid down the wall and held up a creased contract that had been lying abandoned on the floor. "We would have a home," he said, his voice low. "The other day I read that some kids set fire to a vamp hiding in an abandoned building."

"We took this way of life to live outside of society. Vincent's offering us a prison. We'll be a freak show."

"We won't have to hunt. No more drones. We'll be with others like us. He promises us a lot."

Sylvie faced the wall. "I could go home."

Raoul cupped her chin, his long nails caressing her cold skin. "They're all dead, honey. They died a hundred years ago. We have no more home, and we are running out of options."

"It's … it's inhumane, what they want to do."

"I told you … we have no choice."

Raoul stood, holding his hand out. Sylvie allowed him to haul her up. She was hungry and chilled. Vincent promised them a haven, a place to thrive. It was time to come out of the cold.

Chapter 4

Wyatt pulled into the designated area for employee parking. He was early, but then he always was early. It was his passenger, Melvin Riley, who pressed the boundaries.

Melvin was Wyatt's first friend in Copper Valley. Most of the kids were wary of the newcomer and did everything in their power to exclude him from activities. Melvin lived with his grandfather in a run-down ranch and was rarely included in anything. Socially awkward, his preoccupation with space invaders, werewolves, and horror movies of the 50's, *Creature from the Black Lagoon* his favorite, made him as unpopular as Wyatt. Still, he was kind, honest, and loyal. Wyatt befriended him and found himself, more often than not, protecting his newfound friend, often the target of the school bullies.

Melvin was smart, his interests varied, and he was entertaining. Lately, though, their fun had gotten boring. Wyatt might be spending time with Melvin, but he wished he were with Jade instead.

"Take your apron," Wyatt told him as he got out of the car, admonishing him as if he were a child. It was getting to be a burden, taking care of him. You had to remind Melvin of everything.

He had to admit that Melvin could be off-putting because of his social awkwardness. Still, he made sure never to leave him out. Wyatt was positive being with Melvin prevented a level of acceptance from the other kids. While some did like Wyatt, nobody enjoyed Melvin's company.

Melvin dropped a notebook, spilling his chemistry worksheets all over the passenger side of the car. "Dang it!" Melvin cursed.

Melvin was a hot mess, from his T-shirt hanging over his pants to the mismatched expressions and his thrift shop clothing choices. Acne still ravaged his face, and, as if that wasn't enough, he had been cursed with frizzy auburn hair. He wore a fake gold werewolf head pendant with bright emerald glass eyes on a clunky, thick chain around his neck. Wyatt knew it had to be ten years old. He had thrown out a very similar one that he'd had in a box at the bottom of his closet at home. It had gone the way of his Super Mario Brothers game and Hulk Hogan action figure. Everybody wore werewolf heads when they were younger. He told his friend it was time to put it away, but it was as much a part of Melvin as his hazel eyes.

It would be a miracle if that kid ever got laid, Wyatt thought. Not that Wyatt had, but he was hopeful. He often wondered if Melvin even noticed. He was always buried in his computer, continually accumulating as much information as his brain could handle.

Melvin had made CalTech with a full scholarship, and this would be the last summer they would be together. He worried if people would accept the odd boy when he moved into the dorms. Wyatt was going to a local community college. His parents couldn't afford tuition anywhere else.

His father, the fancy LA lawyer, had left all his money to a charity, which, while very noble, kind of irritated Wyatt as well. It was a mean thing to do to his kids, taking out the messy divorce on his offspring. *Well, beggars can't be choosers,* he thought to himself.

"Mel ..." Wyatt tried hard not to get annoyed. He leaned back in, reaching forward to help his friend pick up the scattered notes. "Gonzales is going to be pissed if she sees your worksheets like this."

"I was going to organize it at work."

"When? While you work at the window? You want to get fired?"

Melvin shrugged. "They need us more than we need them. We have a symbiotic relationship. If Instaburger fires us, who's going to serve—werewolves?"

This was a long-running feud between them. When news broke of the werewolf colony, Melvin made it his mission to advocate their superiority to anyone who would listen. Wyatt liked to spar against Melvin's monster of choice by promoting the value of the zombie population. At least they were human —well, sort of human.

"Impossible. They'd eat all the meat," Wyatt told him. He was getting tired of this debate. It was time to leave it in the recess of his childhood.

"And a zombie wouldn't? The vampires would suck it dry. We've got them by the balls. They don't have a choice."

Wyatt laughed. "Yeah, sure."

Melvin hiked his notebook, papers trailing behind him, under his arm. "Which brings me back to our discussion. I want to add that the werewolf's developed sense of smell makes him the sure winner."

Wyatt shook his head. "What planet are you on? Zombies are like those long-lasting batteries—they keep ticking."

"Ha," Melvin laughed. "Until they start dining on their own body parts. They're mindless, infected, eating machines that can't tell a Ring Ding from a ding-a-ling." He pointed to his crotch. "Besides, werewolves have a normal nervous system."

"Big deal." Wyatt waved his arm in dismissal. "One bite from a zombie and the person is instantly infected. Werewolves have to bite when the moon is full and the mood is right. Like, Sinatra has to be on or something."

"Frank Sinatra? Are you kidding me? You don't know anything about werewolves." Melvin hefted his books on his hip. "The full moon thing is a myth, some can change at will. Werewolves have epic strength. Zombies have weak grip, and if a zombie's leg is broken, they're not catching a werewolf." He paused, taking Wyatt's arm. "Listen, Wy, zombies are all defense. Werewolves are offense."

Wyatt looked at his friend. They had been having this discussion for more than half of twelfth grade. He smiled and then replied, "They're just plain offensive. Defense always wins the game."

Melvin rushed ahead of him, pushing through the doors to find Howard Drucker wearing an Instaburger paper hat while wiping the stainless steel countertops. "Quick … Howard Drucker, werewolves versus vampires versus zombies. Who wins?" Everyone always called Howard by his first and last name. Howard made up the last third of their awkward trio.

"You kidding me? The vampire." Howard had curly black hair that hung in a thick mass around his oval head, and he wore heavy horn-rimmed glasses that might have looked good on a tech geek. On Howard, they made him look small, like a cartoon character.

He was the shortest of the group, with a skinny, concave chest. His short stature could have made Howard a victim of the ever-present bullies in school, but his razor tongue was deadlier than a vampire's fangs. Howard never backed down from anything.

"I told you he would say that," Wyatt said confidently. He

opened the gate, coming around to his spot behind the counter.

"This simply is not true," Melvin insisted. He went on, oblivious to the patron waiting for Howard to put her meal together.

"Look, vampires are highly reflexive. Werewolves are intelligent. I'll give you that," Howard said as he packed the meal.

Melvin grinned evilly at Wyatt.

"But zombies ..." Howard continued, "barely functional. Vampire wins."

"Vampires are almost extinct. Werewolves have night vision," the woman said as she scooped her bag off the counter.

"True. But vampires have dilated night vision, and they can grow in number if they want to," he called after her as she left the restaurant, his voice growing louder as she got farther away. "Zombies ... extreme myopia. Once again, vampire wins. Even if there are just a few of them left, they are the thinking man's monsters. One vamp is worth a hundred zombies." He gave a satisfied smile. The door slammed shut. "It's a shame they won't allow them to populate anymore," Howard said "Soon they will disappear like the dinosaurs."

"I guess vampire wins," Wyatt said with resignation.

"You wimp, you gonna give up just like that?" Manny Lopez shouted as he snapped his fingers under Wyatt's nose. He was a twenty-year old college dropout who was now looking at a career as the night manager of Instaburger. Manny was shorter, with a meaner tongue than Howard. "If you are gonna give up like that, you can work the fryer tonight."

"Ugh, the fryer." Wyatt hated working the fryer. The oil spat, and the lamps that kept the fries hot were scorching. "I stand by my opinion; zombies are superior. When aroused, they're unstoppable."

"Okay, Howard Drucker, you have the fryer," Manny informed him.

Howard shook his head. "Vampires have brains and working opposable thumbs. As I said before, they are the thinking man's monster."

"Good man. Melvin, take the fryer."

"Why do I have to work the fryer?" Melvin whined. He blamed it for his acne. His workers' comp case had been closed when they discovered that eating the fries, rather than the splattering oil, caused his condition.

"Because any moron who thinks a werewolf will win should have to do the dirtiest job in the house."

"Dang it." Mel scratched his greasy head.

Howard caught Wyatt's attention and pointed to a silver pickup truck pulling into the parking lot. He went in the back to work the burger assembly line. Wyatt turned, dismay written across his face as multiple car doors slammed, and a group strolled into the restaurant.

There were four of them: Nolan, the beefy captain of the football team; Theo, his best friend; plus two girls from school, Jade and Keisha. Wyatt cursed softly, taking his place behind register one.

"Put on your hat," Manny admonished him. "Melvin, take out the trash and stop stuffing your face with the fries!"

Nolan walked up to the counter, his gait lazy, as if he didn't have a care in the world. He was tall, with wide shoulders and short cut blond hair. "I don't know about you," he thundered, "but I am *desperate* for a good burger." He drew out the word "desperate" slowly.

Wyatt opened his mouth to say something snarky to the jock and then considered the nasty possibilities of Nolan's response. Nolan was as hot-tempered as he was reactive. He was known to sucker punch teammates when they disagreed with his football calls. Wyatt wisely decided to keep quiet.

"Oh, look who?" Nolan acted surprised. "Wyatt Baldwin. Are you *desperate* to sell me a burger?"

Wyatt's heart sank; he could feel the shame of the note on his back again. He wished he'd taken the fryer duty after all.

Jade and Keisha approached the counter, smiling at Wyatt.

"What did Casella give you for your paper?" Keisha asked.

"I got an A." Wyatt shrugged, his voice low as if he were ashamed.

"Me too. It was easy," Keisha replied. She was tall, with long legs and a curly Afro held back from her lovely face with two barrettes. She had slanted dark eyes and wide lips with a friendly smile. She was head of the cheerleading squad and the smartest girl in school. Wyatt grinned when he heard the clumsy clatter of Howard dropping a metal pan. He wasn't the only klutz in the restaurant. It was followed by a muffled curse. Keisha liked Howard, but she couldn't get him to do anything more than stare at her.

"Is that you, Howard Drucker?" Keisha called. "Come out here so I can see you!"

"Who's going to cook your burger if I come out there?" Howard grumbled.

Jade gazed at Wyatt with a sweet smile. She toyed with a hank of her brown hair, twirling it until it fell like a fat sausage on her shoulder. Nolan and Jade had been on-again, off-again since fifth grade.

Wyatt looked at her and admitted wryly to himself that he was indeed quite *desperate* to catch her on the off-again loop. When he was around her, his throat turned into a noose, and words had to be painfully squeezed out. Wyatt swallowed hard, looking at her perfect teeth as she bit her lower lip. She was lightly tanned, but she glowed when she walked into a room. Keisha and Jade were dressed in tennis skirts. Keisha shoved her shoulder into Jade's, playfully smiling.

Wyatt's face turned crimson. Jade had picked him to do a

33

report on the containment camps this spring, and she worked with him on a community project for the homeless. They had to meet alone to write the paper. It was probably the highlight of his senior year. It was like she was finding excuses to be with him.

Wyatt opened his mouth to say something but found his vocal cords uncooperative.

Nolan was oblivious to the interplay and pounded his chest. "Me want meat." He came forward, wrapping one arm around Jade's waist, picking her up. "Me want meat."

Theo walked over to Keisha, who eyed him sideways. "Don't even think about it," she told him pointedly. "I could crush you like the vermin you are."

"*Ay caramba*, Mamacita," Manny crooned. "You too harsh on that boy. Maybe you need a real man."

Keisha rolled her eyes, dismissing him. "Keep that up, Manny, and I'll have to show you what I learned in taekwondo this week."

"Yeah, man, she threw the instructor over her shoulder. You better watch out," Theo said in a stage whisper.

"Howard Drucker! Make me a Double-Wubble the way I like it. You know the way I like it, don't you? You still wearing your pocket protector?" Keisha asked seductively.

"Aw, leave him alone, Keisha," Wyatt murmured. "You'll make him nervous."

"What? I think it's sexy. All loaded up with number two pencils and his compass. His weapons of choice," she said with a smile. "Maybe he's got other goodies stuffed in that thing."

This time something very big and probably expensive hit the floor. Nolan and Theo roared with laughter. Jade caught Wyatt's flushed face again, and Manny cursed loudly, running to the back, muttering about kids.

Theo saw a dusty black Sprinter pull up and wandered to the window to investigate. He called to Nolan to see if he recognized the vehicle. Nolan pulled Jade possessively with him to the window. She hung backward; Nolan gave her a look of warning, and she stood just to the side of him.

Wyatt leaned over the counter, swallowing hard, and then, taking a deep breath, he asked Keisha, "Why'd you do that to Howard Drucker? You know he likes you."

Keisha made a rude noise. "Well," she huffed. "When you like someone enough, you should ask them to go out to a movie or something." She propped herself on the counter, so she was half on it, her long legs dangling. "Don't you agree, Howard Drucker?" she shouted. "That goes for you too," Keisha said in an undertone to Wyatt and then glanced over her shoulder at Jade.

Wyatt looked nervously away, his fingers fidgeting with a paper bag. He peeked up to find Jade's steady gaze upon him.

Jade was back, her face intent as if she were trying to tell him something. Or maybe that was his imagination speaking, and she was just nice. *If she was even slightly interested in me,* he thought bitterly, *why was she hanging around King Kong?*

Both girls jumped back with loud shrieks when Melvin appeared out of the darkness to stack a tray with fresh fries. His face floated between the shelves, the light painting it with an eerie reddish glow. The green glass of his werewolf pendant winked in the steam.

Wyatt dragged his eyes from Jade and laughed. "It's just Melvin." He turned around and said to his friend, "Mel, you should see what you look like."

"What? What do I look like?"

"Like the star attraction at Monsterland, that's what," Keisha said. "You should make a little noise when you approach people. You're a scary dude."

"Me? Scary? You think so?" Melvin was impressed. "Did you hear that, Wy? I gotta see that in the mirror. I'm taking a break."

Melvin rushed toward the restroom, Jade waved her

fingers and said, "Hi Melvin." She turned to Keisha and commented, "He's not that scary."

"He's so weird," Keisha said to Wyatt. "Why do you hang out with him?"

Wyatt shrugged. "Maybe I should wonder why he hangs out with me. Maybe we're the weird ones."

Keisha's mouth dropped open. "I think you just blew my mind."

"What? Who blew what?" Nolan was back, rapping out an order. He sized up Wyatt. "I heard Vincent Konrad gave all the civil servants free tickets for the opening of Monsterland," he said contemptuously.

"So?"

"Did your father score?"

"Who?"

"Carter White, your father."

"My stepfather Carter? Um ... no. He's not interested. He—"

"Yeah?"

"He's not happy about the park."

"What's that got to do with it? If you had them, I'd offer a thousand for two. Right, Jade, you want to go?"

"Hey," Theo said. "If you were going to Monsterland, that extra ticket would be for me, bro."

Nolan's eyes narrowed at Jade, who was watching Wyatt. He put his arms around her back to grip her shoulder. She tried to ease out of his hold, but he held her tight. "Don't think so. I'd want my girl to be with me." He gave her a slight shake. "Right, Jade?"

Jade tore her gaze from Wyatt to look at Nolan and then to the floor. Her mumbled answer was cut off when the door flew open, and the room flooded with a group of people. They were not from around here. Wyatt stared at them, not recognizing them. There were no strangers in Copper Valley—well, except for the homeless. With a population of barely twelve hundred, a person grew up knowing everybody else in the small town.

About ten people were filing in, Los Angeles types with smartphones and tablets; most were dressed in grungy, black-colored clothes covered with reddish dust. They were filthy, as if they had been working in the old copper mines.

A girl approached the counter. Her skin was fish-belly white, her hair an unnatural magenta. It was spiked around her small head. She asked Nolan impatiently, "Are you done ordering? I have a large order." She turned around and shouted, "Ryan, you wanted a bun, no meat, right? But you'll eat cheese?"

"I'm lactose intolerant," the only man in the group wearing a business suit whined. "A bun with tomato and lettuce."

"May I have your name for the order please," Wyatt asked.

"Sharice," she replied.

Sharice's group settled around four tables, their heads together, deep in conversation. "I want that too! I can't look at meat anymore," a girl on the far end of the crowd called out.

The door opened again, and a shabby man with a long khaki-colored coat slid into a dark corner. A vagrant, Wyatt surmised. *Who wore a coat in the summer,* Wyatt wondered, observing him. *Someone who had no place to leave it, who didn't belong anywhere,* he thought, looking at the bum, who hunched himself down, his hair covering his lean face. Wyatt knew that feeling well. He watched the hungry eyes dart around the room until they settled on him. He seemed familiar, but Wyatt couldn't place him.

Manny tended to be mean to the homeless, but Wyatt felt a keen sense of responsibility. These people were the real victims of the outbreak. His mother regularly gave out meals to anyone who passed by. Carter donated old clothes. Vincent Konrad's mission was to put them on their feet again by creating jobs. The mogul was proactively finding solutions, he had argued with Carter. At least, unlike the polarized politicians in Washington, he was doing something to help the country. Wyatt even explained in school that, if everyone did a little something to help, the problem would solve itself.

He heard Manny curse when he spied the dirty-looking man. The manager passed Wyatt and quietly said, "Tell him to leave."

"He's not disturbing anybody, Manny. Give the guy a break. It's hot outside."

"If it's so hot, why's he dressed like the Grim Reaper?" With disgust, Manny eyed the leather duster the man wore.

Wyatt finished ringing up Nolan's order, quickly packaging it.

"Have a heart, Manny. Maybe he's a vet." Carter was a veteran. His stepfather always talked about returning soldiers, friends who fell on hard times.

"If he's a vet, he musta been one from the Crusades."

Wyatt smiled, knowing Manny was joking, so he was okay with it. He watched the old guy looking down, trying to be inconspicuous, as if he wanted to disappear. Wyatt recognized that feeling. "Let it go, Manny," he said in a small voice.

Manny shrugged. "Okay, Wyatt, but he makes a mess, you have to clean it up."

Nolan swiped his bag from the counter and headed for the door. Jade pulled his hand, her voice imploring, "I want to eat inside."

Nolan gave in ungraciously, and the four of them took a booth in the rear. The restaurant was packed now—burgers were flying; stacks of fries and a dozen shakes were all carried over to the large group of newcomers. The noise level rose, the group bickering about something. *They must be here for the theme park*, Wyatt figured.

He turned, looking at the older man who sat drumming his fingers uncomfortably. His shoes were caked with mud, and the coat's hem rested on the floor. The patrons treated him as though he were invisible. Wyatt pulled out a few bucks from his pocket and placed it in the register. Employees ate half price. Wyatt took a Double-Wubble, a large package of fries, and a shake and brought it over to the bum.

"Where are you goin' with that?" Manny called out with exasperation, watching Wyatt place it on the table where the man sat alone. "If you feed him, he'll keep coming back."

"Don't worry. I paid for it," Wyatt told him quietly over his shoulder. The shyness he felt around his peers evaporated. Wyatt understood loneliness, the malaise of not fitting in. While he was tongue-tied with Jade or a bully like Nolan, his sense of compassion took over for someone down on their luck. It was these qualities that drew Melvin and Howard Drucker to him. He never judged, and he wanted so much to make people feel at ease around each other. "Hungry?" he asked.

The huge group grew strangely quiet. The lactose intolerant man wearing the suit stood. He had his mouth open to interrupt Wyatt, but something unseen to everyone else made him pause.

"Is that for me?" the old man asked softly.

"It's the best burger we have." He leaned down to confide. "I like it better than the fish, but if you'd rather—"

"I didn't pay for it." He considered Wyatt, his eyes piercingly direct. "Do you know who I am?"

Wyatt searched his face but couldn't place him. He was painfully skinny, his cheekbones jutting from his face, the creases lined with the red dust of the valley. He shook his head. "Doesn't matter. My name's Wyatt. Don't worry about the cost. My treat," Wyatt said as he gestured to the food on the table. "I've got another for you when you leave … for later."

"No, no, this is fine, I mean exceptional. You're very

kind." He glanced back at Sharice and the group in silent communication. "What's your last name?"

"Baldwin, sir. My name is Wyatt Baldwin."

"Baldwin. Baldwin. I knew a Baldwin once."

"It's a pretty common name, sir. And you're probably thinking of Alec, Stephen, or Billy—the family of actors. No relation. What's yours?" Wyatt held out his hand.

"If you touch that guy, I don't want you touching my food!" Nolan shouted.

Wyatt ignored Nolan, reaching forward to take the grubby hand. "Don't pay attention to him."

"You're very brave," the man stated. "Do you always shake a stranger's hand?"

"If we've shaken hands, I don't think we're strangers anymore. Besides, I've introduced myself."

"Indeed, you have," the man said, coming to his feet, straightening up. He was so tall, Wyatt had to put his head back to look up to him. *He didn't look old or frail after all,* Wyatt thought. His black eyes swept the room, coming back to rest on Wyatt. "Doctor Vincent Konrad," the man replied, taking Wyatt's hand in a surprisingly strong handshake. "Forgive my filth. We've been knee deep in your red sand, getting the park ready. The werewolves ..." he said as if it were an apology. "You understand." His deep voice filled the room, and Wyatt was awed by his presence.

Wyatt's eyes widened with excitement as he looked closely at the man's lined face. He was dirty, his hair scraggly, but the eyes—*Vincent Konrad in Instaburger?* Wyatt was thrilled with the thought of it. Meeting him was unbelievable, a dream come true. Wyatt smiled; that's why he seemed familiar. His face split into a wide grin. He pumped the older man's hand enthusiastically. "Dr. Konrad! You look so ... different. This is amazing." He pulled his phone from his back pocket. "Do you mind if we take a selfie? No one is going to believe this," he said, his voice cracking.

Vincent smiled, leaning toward Wyatt's shoulder to squeeze into the frame.

"How's it going down there? Are you ready for the opening?" Rapid-fire questions popped out of Wyatt's mouth. He was standing right next to him, the most famous man in the country, now the planet. He had treated Vincent Konrad to a Double-Wubble. *Wait till I tell Carter,* Wyatt thought, his eyes bright with excitement. "Man, what I would give to go to the park tomorrow," Wyatt said.

"Really?" Vincent turned to look at him full in the face. "What would you give?"

Nolan burst out laughing, "Yeah, that's Vincent Konrad, like I'm Tom Brady," he sneered.

Sharice's group stopped talking at once. The room was silent, except for Nolan's inappropriate laughter. Vincent snapped his fingers and then held up four fingers.

Sharice fiddled with different envelopes. Vincent turned a baleful eye on her, and her search became frantic. Dropping her sheaf of papers, she rushed to him, slapping four silver strips into his palm, uttering an apology.

Vincent walked deliberately to the table in the rear. Nolan's laughter died on his lips, his face puzzled.

"Ah, the cool kids. So you don't believe that I am Vincent Konrad?" he asked with menacing calm. "I wonder, what will it take for you to believe? Do you like to be scared?" He leaned down, his face next to Jade, who sat frozen in her chair. Theo edged away from the old man. Keisha stared him straight in the face. He wagged a finger at her. "You don't seem afraid of anything." He peeled off one ticket, letting it float onto the greasy tabletop. "One ticket for Diana."

"My name's Keisha."

"I think you are the fair Diana, goddess of the hunt," he said, considering her appreciatively.

Keisha picked up the ticket to look at its contents. Nolan snatched it from her slender fingers. "Hey!"

41

"Holy cow, this is a ticket for the grand opening of Monsterland!" Nolan looked up to reconsider the older man. "You really are Vincent Konrad."

"*Doctor* Vincent Konrad," he corrected. "I need you youngsters to come and take lots of pictures and spread the word using all those little devices you're so addicted to." He dropped the remaining tickets onto the table. "Let's see if Monsterland can scare the daylights out of you." Vincent leered at them.

"These are free tickets," Keisha said suspiciously. "Why are you giving them to us?"

Vincent's eyes bored into Nolan. "What's your name?"

"Nolan Steward." Nolan puffed out his chest and then reached out for a handshake. "My father is—"

"I know who your father is," Vincent eyed his proffered hand and dismissed him.

Jade shuddered. "I don't know—"

"You don't know what?" Vincent moved down to be eye level with her.

"Wyatt was kind. He gave you something to eat. Why would you give Nolan the tickets?"

Vincent's long fingers caressed the top of Jade's head. "Very nice. Very nice. I like a girl with heart." Vincent turned, opening his arms wide. "You are right! It seems as though we have left out the nerds! But …," he rose and circled the room, "appearances can be deceiving," he said grandly. "I have something very special in store for Wyatt of the infamous Baldwins. Perhaps you'll invite Alec?"

Wyatt smiled, shaking his head. "I told you, no relation, Doctor."

Vincent went on as if he hadn't spoken. "Do you have any more presidential passes, Sharice?"

Sharice rifled through a canvas bag that lay on the table, handing Wyatt a large cream-colored scroll. It looked like a diploma, with a red ribbon tied in the center. Wyatt stared at the missive, his heart beating in his chest; the room receded.

"Open it; open the scroll," Vincent said, his voice a husky whisper.

Wyatt slowly unrolled the parchment.

"Make sure you save it. It will be a collector's item someday."

"What's this made of?" Wyatt asked, looking at the calligraphy.

Vincent didn't answer him. Sharice pointed to the second paragraph. "We are only giving these out to the president and the other politicians and dignitaries coming tomorrow. You have a backstage pass to see how the park is run."

Howard stood behind the counter; his jaw opened wide. "Backstage pass?" he asked in wonder. "How many of those did you get, Wyatt?"

"How many do you have, Sharice?" Vincent called over his shoulder.

"Four," she replied, laying three others on the yellow Formica table.

"Excellent, one for each of the generous workers here tonight," Vincent roared. Now he was in his element. Wyatt didn't understand how he could have mistaken him for a bum. Dr. Konrad walked around the room, as if he were hosting a stylish soirée. He wore a broad smile, and his hands were outstretched to embrace the entire room. Vincent Konrad was a modern-day P.T. Barnum. Despite his unkempt appearance, this man could control a crowd. The room was silent, the electricity of Vincent's presence captivating them all. "The price of these tickets is for you to tell the world about Monsterland. You will initiate the planet to the wonders I've created."

"Yeah, us and about ten thousand others," Manny said.

"Shut up, Manny," Nolan responded.

Wyatt eagerly followed him around the room, his body buzzing with anticipation. He looked at the other people, noticing that everyone was captivated by Vincent. Fries sizzled in the oil, forgotten, the bright lights overhead highlighting the feverish glow of the older man's eyes. Wyatt gazed at Vincent's rapt face—a chill danced down his spine. Those eyes were hard, lit as though a fire raged on the inside. Wyatt watched the fathomless black orbs scanning the room, taking note of each person in there. They landed on him, probing so deeply he felt strangely violated, as though Vincent could see his private thoughts. He thought about Carter and his dislike for the mogul. Wyatt shuddered, his hand closing on the scroll, feeling the soft material. He turned it over in his hand and wondered if it were made from a chamois, the sheepskin he used to clean his car.

Wyatt heard Melvin shrieking like a hyena as he danced in the back of the restaurant. The room filled with the stench of burning fries. "We're going to Monsterland … we're going to Monsterland!" Wyatt glanced at Jade and then back to Melvin, who was running around like a whirling dervish. He closed his eyes and, for a minute, thought about holding Jade's hand as they walked through the park. Reality invaded when Melvin ran up panting, "I am so pumped." His voice cracked. Wyatt frowned.

Manny cursed and ran to the back. "My fries!"

With an imperious wave of his hand, Vincent stepped toward the door, stopping to turn and look at the group.

He pointed to Nolan. "You think you are in control. You are not afraid of anything, are you?" he asked in a provocative voice. "Let's see if I have the ability to scare you."

Wyatt looked down at the invitation. It was parchment, he realized. Parchment made of skin. It was some kind of animal skin. He felt the urge to drop it.

Vincent put his hand on the door to leave, but Wyatt called out. "Hey!" The doctor stopped to turn around and look at him. Wyatt held the invitations loosely in the palm of his hand. "Monsterland … it's safe, right?"

Vincent laughed, his crew tittering nervously. "Monster-land is the safest place on Earth. I assure you, the safest place. And you will be the ones to tell the world." He swept out of the restaurant.

Wyatt went to the window to watch Vincent's entourage get into the big black Sprinter. He felt Manny next to him, observing as well. He smelled like burnt fries.

"Creepy sucker. Why'd you give him the burger?"

Wyatt shrugged. "He looked hungry." He handed the manager one of the scrolls.

"Yeah, like a wolf."

Wyatt shook his head, not sure at this point. "No, he has this … power. You know … what do they call it? Charisma?" Wyatt said, but, for the first time, doubting exactly what he found so captivating.

"He's a creep," Manny said. "I don't like him or his park. I'm sorry they built it in Copper Valley. Here, take this." He slapped his parchment into Wyatt's hand. He wiped his hands down the sides of his dirty apron as if he touched something foul and filthy.

"No, it's worth money. Sell it."

"I don't want anything to do with Vincent Konrad or Monsterland. Give it to someone."

Wyatt's fist closed around the soft material.

Chapter 5

Shonkin, Montana

The man's fist closed around the cold metal of the fence. He shouldn't have felt anything, but the hard surface of the chain link registered, and he sighed, knowing in some small part of his brain that the infection had now ravaged his thought process.

He opened his mouth, attempting to speak, and nothing emerged but the inhuman grunts indicating the virus had spread to his vocal cords. He tried again, squeezing out a word.

Words were his craft—he couldn't lose that. Tears smarted his eyes; at least they still functioned. His voice, his tool of the trade, was almost gone. He was an eloquent speaker, nimble with words, able to twist and mold concepts into believable ideas.

Now he communicated with a one-note groan that no one understood, and it seemed only to gain him another portion of the bloody gruel they sent in through long pipelines.

He stared bleakly through the slats of the fence. It was

covered with a privacy screen, shielding the outside world from the horror that was his life.

He poked the hard metal, his finger breaking off to land with a dull thud at his feet. He looked upward with despair, the constant drag of feet telling him they heard his appendage drop. He gagged, smelling them as they approached, their disease more advanced, their bodies rotting on their frames.

Most were missing parts—an eye here, an arm there. Some teetered on stumps—all that was left of their legs. Usually, by then, all reason was gone; their eyes were vacant, filmed over with a white substance; gray matter leaked from their ears, and they moved with mindless intent—brainless creatures, waiting to be put out of their misery with a final blow to their fragile heads.

There was a fight over his finger. He didn't even try to retrieve it. He watched in disgust as two men tore at each other for the prize morsel. They shouldn't be fighting over flesh, some small part of his mind reasoned.

They were fed regularly. Usually, it was recycled food from institutions, refuse they used to feed the hogs. Someone had to feed the plague victims before they fed on each other. He stood back, some shred of his long-lost humanity making his gorge rise. He backed away as the two fighters slugged it out over his fleshy finger. He heard the splat of their soupy skin hitting each other, the splatter of discased bone and blood flying around the corner of the compound to scatter on the hard dirt.

He had traveled into the danger zone even though he was advised against it. He had to research for his job. It was safe, he was told. You could touch them. It was body fluids that were the problem, they assured him. After all, legions of people were there taking care of the infected. Hours after he returned, he woke from a nap to find his skin sagging, turning soft like warm putty. His face changed—his cheekbones jutting out, his skin hanging, shredding when touched. It hurt to breathe, yet he lived. They came for him, locking him in the internment camp to feed or be fed.

For a few months, he had lived here, never appreciating his former life, never understanding what he had so casually tossed away, waiting for death to claim him. All he'd ever cared about was his career, and, ultimately, it had killed him.

There was no cure, of this he was sure. No treatment, no hope, just the endless hunger for flesh, any meat he could devour to try to feed the relentless hunger that gnawed at him from the depths of hell from which it came.

Chapter 6

Gracie White pressed a cool hand to her throbbing head. Wyatt and Sean were fighting again. She could hear their shouts all the way into the kitchen. They had been like this for the last year. She tried so hard to teach them the right things. She couldn't understand it. They were always close as children. Wyatt had watched out for his younger brother, especially when Frank was moody. Recently, things had gotten terrible. They couldn't be in a room for five minutes without a fight. It was like she didn't recognize them.

When Frank and she split, the boys were younger, and she tried to shield them from the acrimonious divorce. Frank had stripped her of everything, using an airtight prenuptial agreement. She struggled on the pittance her ex-husband was able to negotiate. *What a mess,* Gracie thought with a bitter laugh. In truth, she was so happy to be out of the marriage, she didn't care.

All Frank ever cared about was work, no matter what lies he fed them. Well, he could keep his mid-century modern in the Hollywood Hills, as well as the girlfriend he kept in a condo he didn't know she knew about in Studio City. "Do you know why divorce is so expensive?" her lawyer asked her early on. "Because it's worth it," he answered with a laugh.

Frank was a high-priced attorney in Los Angeles and used a friend to make the ridiculous settlement. Moving to Copper Valley, her old hometown, infuriated her ex, but she needed to regroup. He'd cut the boys off completely, threw them away like yesterday's trash, seeing them only for a few weeks last summer. Claimed he didn't have time. He told them he was working on something big. Then he died, but of course, the boys didn't know the circumstances.

The house vibrated with the impact of a door slamming. *Oh no, they're at it again*, like two wrestlers in a ring. She was going to have to go back there and separate them. Gracie put the masher on the counter, her hand still resting on the bowl of potatoes. The butter melted into a yellow river between the half-smashed lumps. Wiping her hands on a dishrag, she turned to leave the kitchen when the back door opened and Carter walked in.

"Pork chops?" he asked, his dark hair tousled. "You okay?" He slipped his gun onto the top of the cabinet over the sink. "Ah ..." he commented as another bout of shouting ensued. "Have you heard any bodies hitting the floor?"

He reached forward to take her into his arms. She fit perfectly beneath his chin, her body tense. He rubbed her back and then looked up when a thud shook the walls. "I'll get them."

"No, I'll do it." Gracie stopped herself when she saw the hurt flit across his face. He was trying so hard to bond with them. She cocked her head. "You sure?"

"I got it." He kissed her lightly on the lips. Gracie heard his feet navigate the small house followed by his knock on their bedroom door. The shouting stopped.

Carter complained that the boys treated him as if he was temporary, like a rental. She hated that they'd clam up, their faces bordering on anger when he disciplined them. She knew her sons liked him; however, blending the family into a unit had proven a lot harder in practice than in theory.

Carter was a world of difference from their father. He was a good man—fair, kind, not flashy, the salt of the earth. In other words, the exact opposite of their father. He was a damn sight better parent than Frank ever was, but time dulled the disappointments, leaving the memories rosy and sentimental.

She didn't get it. Frank had practically abandoned them and bankrupted her, forcing her to find a job in her old hometown, leaving Los Angeles and their privileged life behind them. In the end, he barely saw the kids; he was traveling too much for his client. She knew nothing more.

Frank was secretive and greedy, leaving her to fend for herself and support the kids. Initially, she thought he was doing that so he could get custody, but she soon realized he didn't give a crap about them at all. Maybe it was better the boys didn't understand that. What good would come out of them feeling abandoned?

She craned her neck, listening intently, but couldn't hear anything. She had asked the kids to call Carter *Dad*, but they creatively managed to call him anything but that. Maybe they'd start calling him *Dad* soon.

She laid the platter of meat on the kitchen table and went back to mashing the potatoes. It was quiet in the house, and, by the time she was placing the mountain of steaming string beans on the serving dish, she heard the stomping of three sets of feet making their way into the hot kitchen.

The kitchen grew cramped as the adult-sized males filed into the room. Wyatt grabbed his chair, Sean had a toothy smile, and Carter's face was unreadable.

"Sharing is caring," Gracie said, expecting an explanation.

"That's what I'm talking about!" Sean shouted. "See, I told you."

Gracie eyed Carter, her head cocked in question. "So?"

Carter held his hand out for the mashed potatoes to be passed to him. He looked at Wyatt with raised eyebrows.

"I don't think it's fair," Wyatt said. "Look, it's my ticket."

"I told you how we are going to handle it."

"You're not my father! I don't have to do what you say."

"Wyatt!" Gracie said. "Apologize this instant to your dad."

Carter scrutinized him.

It wasn't that they didn't like Carter; it felt unnatural, they kept telling their mom. While their father had not been the father of the year, he was still their dad, Wyatt always reminded her.

"Sorry," Wyatt said, and then added, "Carter."

Gracie sighed, and Carter stopped her with a gentle hand. "It's good enough, Grace."

"Look, I can't give an opinion if I don't know what happened," Gracie said.

"I … Vincent Konrad came into work today."

"What … Instaburger?"

"Yeah, well … he has to eat, right?" Wyatt said defensively.

Gracie shuddered. "I'm surprised. I guess I never expected him to eat at a place like that."

"More'n likely he eats the same swill as the zombies," Carter commented.

"He's okay," Wyatt replied. "He's more than okay—he's a humanitarian."

"I wouldn't go that far," Carter said.

"He's the best!" Sean half stood from his place with excitement.

"Settle down, Sean." Carter nodded.

Sean hopped from foot to foot. "Listen to your dad," Gracie told him.

Both boys looked at her but said nothing. Sean remained standing.

"What did he do?" Gracie broke the silence and put more beans on Sean's plate.

"Aw, Ma," Wyatt whined at her stern expression.

"He gave Wyatt four free tickets, and I want the extra one," Sean crowed.

"Tickets ... to Monsterland? I thought we talked about that." Gracie put down her fork. She turned to Carter. "We didn't take the tickets he offered to all the town workers. No ... I won't allow it."

"Mom!" both boys said at once.

Wyatt was first. "I don't know why you don't want to let us go. He gave me a special pass, one that would allow us behind the scenes, to see how the park works."

"Yeah!"

"It's a once-in-a-lifetime chance," Wyatt added.

"He has four invitations!" Sean shouted.

"Shut up, Sean," Wyatt said.

"Wyatt ..." Carter warned.

Wyatt's cheeks grew red with frustration. He continued, his voice slightly elevated. "He gave me special VIP passes. He said it was safe. The mayor, senator, and governor are going to be there."

"President McAdams too," Carter said, and then added, "and me."

"You?" Gracie looked miserable.

"We've all been called in. Jessup's even bringing in volunteers. We're not equipped to handle the level of people attending."

"Dr. Konrad should supply his own guards," Gracie said, biting her lower lip.

"He is," Carter placated her. "He is supplying them at all seven of the parks. He has his global opening tomorrow. Monsterland is the biggest thing to hit the planet." He shrugged, his face unhappy. "Look, Grace, once the president said he was attending, they had to pull out all the stops."

"It's like being part of history. I have to go. Vincent Konrad asked us to be his ambassadors to tell the world about Monsterland," Wyatt said.

"Carter," Gracie implored.

"I agree with you, but Grace …" He looked her full in the face. "It's safe. Konrad's got it all under control." He glanced at the eager boys and then back at her. "I'd rather they got it out of their systems on a day when security will be high than a regular day. Besides, I'll be there as well."

Gracie still wasn't happy. "What was the fight about?"

"Manny gave me an extra ticket. Brian Ferguson offered me five hundred dollars for it."

"You're not scalping a ticket," Carter said, looking at his stepson. "You might as well give it to Sean."

"See." Sean beamed. "I'm going to Monsterland. Thanks, Carter."

"Yeah, thanks, Carter," Wyatt said rolling his eyes.

"They can watch out for each other," Carter said with a shrug. He made eye contact with Wyatt. "Are we okay?"

"Do I have a choice?"

Carter said a quiet, "No."

The room grew dark as twilight moved in. They heard the sound of the wolves howling miles away. Sean rose to turn on the light to chase the shadows from the kitchen.

Gracie's lips tightened. "You'll be home early?"

"Early in the morning," Sean said.

"What do you mean, early in the morning?"

Wyatt put down his fork and knife, calmly stating, "The park opens at sunset, Mom."

Gracie raised her eyebrows at Carter. "Sunset?" her voice squeaked.

"I'll be working." Carter stood up bringing his plate to the sink. "I'll be there, Gracie," he said, and the subject was closed.

Chapter 7

"You don't expect me to live this way?" Sylvie threw down the plastic packet of blood so that it leaked sluggishly on the Styrofoam dishes they used in the commissary exhibit.

It was a mock restaurant in the Vampire Village. Nobody could eat with the zombies, and nobody wanted to eat with the werewolves. "I can't eat with these things on." She gestured disgustedly at her capped fangs. It was late in the day, and they had all just woken up. The windows had been blackened to keep out the hot desert sunlight.

"Come on, baby," Raoul pleaded. "It will only be for a little while. They said things would improve when money starts pouring in."

"I don't know why we have to wait," she said with a sneer.

"Vincent Konrad is the richest man in the world. He promised us a better existence," Angie complained. She considered the handful of vamps contemptuously, watching them suck on their packets in the dining room. She turned her attention to the guard standing by the exit. She had been recruited in New York, along with four others. She was tall with long legs and had ivory-colored hair. Her pupils were vertical like a cat's, and they glowed with an inner light. She started to rise from the table.

"Where are you going?" Ian stared glumly at his plate. He was Asian, with straight purple hair that covered half his face. They were living together in the rooms above the park.

Angie smirked. "Dessert," she said.

Sylvie and Raoul looked up, their argument stalled, watching Angie circle the guard, who ignored her. She leaned against the wall, smiling coyly at him. He smiled back but turned his face straight ahead.

"She can't do that," Sylvie said, with a shake of her pink curls. "What about her caps?"

"Watch her," Ian responded with a cunning grin, his fangs evident.

"Where are yours?" Sylvie whispered.

"Look. If you leverage your fork just so ..." He pushed the tines of a fork against a lever on the side of her mouth. She felt the brace pop. "Voilà," Ian said with a flourish, holding the offending plastic caps in the palm of his hand. "Just slide them in for inspection. They'll never know." He sucked on his packet, the blood dripping from the corner of his mouth. "I hate mystery blood. Ugh, what is this stuff?"

"It's better than the fish blood they gave us last week." Sylvie made a face, sliding the caps into her pocket.

"It sent those two guys from Nashville to the infirmary. I haven't seen them since." Ian threw down the half-filled packet with revulsion. "They can't expect us to survive on this. We have to do something."

"Like what?" Raoul asked. "We're practically prisoners."

"Angie's planning something big."

"She's satiating her hunger, nothing more. She's selfish. I wish we were placed in the Paris park."

"Ooh, la la. Aren't you fancy." Ian snickered. "Do you think they serve wine with the blood over there? I heard they are getting the same garbage."

"Angie's just a flirt. She wants all the men for herself," Sylvie said with malice.

"A lot you know. She's staging a revolution, one guard at a time," Ian laughed. "There she goes."

"What are you talking about?"

Slowly, Angie moved closer. They could hear her giggling as if the guard made a joke. She inched to his side, whispering something in his ear. Angie disappeared behind the door, the guard leaving a second after her.

"Clever," Raoul said with appreciation.

"It's against the rules!" Sylvie protested.

"Angie doesn't follow the rules," Ian said.

Raoul looked at Ian and asked, "Are you okay with that? You don't get jealous?"

"As long as there is no kissing, I can tolerate it."

"What will she do with the body?" Sylvie murmured.

"She's not going to kill him. She'll get him in a spot where nobody will see it. See that sanitation worker there?" He pointed to a uniformed worker cleaning out a trash can. "She got to him a week ago. He's a drone too. The cafeteria lady, the maintenance workers … she's working her way through the entire staff," Ian said.

Raoul shook his head. "She's jeopardizing it for all of us." He was fiddling with the lock on his caps. They heard the familiar pop, and he smiled as he slid them off. "Ah … what a relief."

Ian lowered his voice. "Look, she's got the right idea. I think we should drone them all. Think of it as insurance. I'm not too sure about Vincent Konrad." Ian looked around the room. "I don't trust him. He hasn't delivered a thing. Aside from that, there were more than two dozen of us in this park when we started. We're down to fifteen now. What happened to those other vamps? I'm thinking of busting out."

"And go where?" Raoul whispered.

"I still have relatives. They are in the blast zone in China;

nobody wants to go there. We could hide out in Shanghai and move our way inland."

"How will we get there from here? We're in the middle of nowhere," Raoul hissed.

Ian rolled his eyes toward the cafeteria worker. "The drones. They'll get us through the desert safely. They know the area."

Raoul gave a slight nod. "It might work. We'd have to travel at night, once the sun's gone down. You have to get one that knows his way around."

"You think?" Ian said, then chuckled.

Raoul agreed. Things had been terrible since they arrived. The doctor oozed charm when he painted a picture of recreating all their former glory. Instead, Vincent Konrad gave them poor reproductions of eighteenth-century clothing, and he stuck them in a sterile version of his concept of East Germany. They were assigned roles in a cheesy rock musical, the music so embarrassingly bad it was more painful to perform it than hear it.

And there was that crazy hunchback he forced into their act. What did he have to do with their image? Raoul had heard a rumor that the good doctor was doing a favor for a celebrity or someone who wanted a relative hidden. *Someone who was rather important,* he thought. It took a lot of gall to place that creature with the vampires. He had a good mind to take it up with the doctor, but lately, Vincent hadn't been seen. He was too busy with his precious openings.

Every bad stereotype was there, making a mockery of their kind. It was supposed to be a place to keep them apart from the population, allowing them to be who they were in a safe environment.

While some found them mysterious, even sexy, Vincent made them into a joke. The show was humiliating. They weren't scary—he didn't revitalize their image. Then there were the forced blood withdrawals.

Vincent started taking their blood—for what, Raoul could only guess. Worse than that, he heard grumblings that Vincent was feeding the werewolves to the zombies and using their skins for parchment. *What kind of monster was he?*

"They'll pick up on it eventually. If you drone too many of them," Raoul said, "Vincent's people will notice the staff has gone passive. If only ..."

"If only what?" Ian looked up, his dark eyes alert.

"If only we could combine forces with the other inmates in the park; we'd outnumber Vincent's people."

"Who needs them?" Ian said. "Werewolves are untamed, and the zombies are so far gone, they're useless."

"Animals can be trained," Raoul retorted.

"Angie's training all the animals we're going to need. Who cares about the others anyway? Once we drone the staff, we'll have an army of allies. It will be the eighties all over again," Ian smirked. "Either way, we are out of here tonight. After I take care of that hunchback."

"Who, Igor? I think he's cute," Sylvie tittered

"You would," Ian sneered.

"Anyway," Sylvie said, "we signed that stupid contract with him. In blood."

"Who cares?" Ian said. "The drones will unlock the gates. We'll slip out after the show."

"Too dangerous." Sylvie eyed the guards nervously.

"So, what are they going to do? Kill us? Last week, he threatened to feed us to the zombies." Ian laughed as he walked toward the door. "Then he can add flesh-eating zombie vampires to his circus."

"Where will you go?" she asked.

"We're heading to the hills southwest of here late tonight. We'll hide there until the sun sets tomorrow and then head west. We've picked two of the drones as slaves ... and nourishment."

"That's one for each of you. Not enough for survival if we go."

"Come with us. Pick a drone of your own, someone who knows the lay of the land."

Raoul became thoughtful. He wasn't comfortable here. He had given up one prison for another. With the right drone, they would find others. They could feed off the community. *China,* he thought with rising excitement. A lot of people in China hadn't been exposed to their music. They may have a shot at something new in a frontier town, away from the tired population of Copper Valley.

Sylvie looked at Raoul. "This place is evil, pure evil. We have to get out of here." It seemed she had the same idea.

Raoul stared toward the distant mountain range. His brain began to percolate.

Chapter 8

Traffic was backed up for miles on the 15. Wyatt, his friends, and his brother Sean had been at a dead stop for over forty-five minutes.

Floodlights lit the long stretch of highway, and enterprising vendors set up road stands, selling T-shirts, water, and fruit. The evening heat was going to be brutal. The radio announcer noted the time was 8:00 p.m. and the freeway to Monsterland was packed tighter than anything they'd seen before.

The teens were surrounded by a variety of license plates. Sean jumped in and out of the car, calling out different states excitedly. Twice Wyatt grumbled for him to get back in the car. All the windows were open, and Wyatt had shut the air conditioning off some time ago. The old clunker appeared dangerously close to overheating.

Police cars raced back and forth over the artificial grass on either side of the roadway. Overhead, a trio of black helicopters made a wide circle in the velvet sky and then started descending.

"Elvis is in the building," Melvin intoned.

"I don't think even Vincent Konrad has the capability of raising someone who's been dead that long," Howard said. "It's McAdams and the senators. This is so disorganized. I told you coming tonight would be a mistake."

Wyatt looked at Howard in the mirror. He was acting strangely. First, Howard gave some lame excuse why he couldn't attend, and then he tried to talk them all out of going. He was jittery and nervous. *Well,* Wyatt thought, *to be honest, Howard Drucker was always tense and nervous, but he appeared more so tonight.*

News crews and their vans lined the median, the large satellites relaying and comparing all the different Monsterland openings. Reporters stood outside, their faces lit by floodlights, mics in hands and stories being told.

Melvin interrupted his thoughts. "He can't raise the dead. Werewolves aren't dead. Vampires technically are undead."

"What's that supposed to mean?" Sean asked.

"Here we go again," Wyatt said, resting his head in his hand. He was getting tired of the argument.

"One doesn't die when they become a vampire; they just live for a longer time or until they get a wooden stake through the heart. Vampires have to be killed by specific means, making people think they are more special than they are."

"As if sucking on blood isn't enough to make someone think you're special," Howard retorted.

"Okay, but zombies are dead," Sean interrupted.

"Go ahead, explain the facts of life to your brother," Howard told Wyatt.

"They're not dead either, just infected with the plague. They are catatonic and have this need to consume flesh, but any meat will do."

"They're zombies," Sean said with a nod.

"Not in the truest sense. They die when you shoot them. Eventually, the illness gets them. That's been the whole problem. They can't live in society because they're out of control. Their brains have been fried by the disease."

"They look like zombies; they smell like zombies—"

"How do you know what they smell like, Sean?" Howard demanded. "When was the last time you rubbed shoulders with one?"

"As a matter of fact, I read about them."

"Yeah, sure."

"Is Carter inside yet?" Melvin asked, interrupting the boys in the backseat.

"He left before three this afternoon," Wyatt responded. He rested his arm out the window. He jerked his hand when it met the burning chrome. "Man, it's hotter than hell out there."

"Idiot," he heard Sean mutter. He glanced at his brother, wondering if Sean was referring to him or Howard Drucker or even Carter. Sean was generally out of charity with everybody.

"Have you heard from him yet?" Howard inquired.

Wyatt shook his head. "Nope." He looked at the sea of cars, wondering where Jade was in the traffic and if he was going to be able to spend any time with her. He sighed.

Howard stuck his head out of the car. "That had to be the president." He sat back down with a groan. "You sure you don't want to turn around?"

"Are you crazy?" Melvin shoved his hand into a package of crispy orange-colored Crux Chips. His upper lip and chin were the same color as his hair.

Melvin sat in the front, and Howard shared the back with the younger boy. A cooler filled with Whisp, their favorite carbonated beverage, was placed between them. They had eaten the sandwiches and were halfway through the snacks.

Wyatt watched Howard in the rearview mirror. His skin was pasty. He had been quiet since he joined them at five o'clock. He tossed his half-eaten candy bar into the trash bag.

"What's the matter with you?" Wyatt asked him quietly.

Melvin fished out the candy bar. "You better finish all that. It says right here." Melvin pointed to his brochure, flakes of Crux Chips landing on his T-shirt. "You can't take any food into the park." His werewolf head necklace was covered with rusty dust. Only the green glass eyes gleamed.

"Despicable," Howard complained. "They control the food concessions so they can charge a fortune for limp bacon and crummy gray burgers. I think it sucks." He pointed to Melvin's pendant. "We chucked those years ago, Mel. Why are you still wearing that?"

Melvin grabbed the snarling werewolf head with his hand. "I love this thing. It's part of my identity. Part of my mojo."

"You don't even know what that means," Howard replied. "You look like a jerk with it."

"You suck!" Melvin retorted. "You afraid of the monsters, Howard Drucker?"

"No, he's afraid of Keisha," Sean laughed.

"Shut up, I'm not scared of anything," Howard responded, his face red. Their shirts stuck to them. They had worn long pants as advised on the news. They were uncomfortable as well as testy. "Can't you put the air back on?" Howard whined.

"Don't think so," Wyatt commented.

"I wish I wore shorts."

"They are trying to keep your limbs safe from the zombies. Carter said they only allow food in hermetically sealed pavilions where it can't be smelled."

"The werewolves' superior sense of smell is no match for a human-made building," Melvin said, his mouth stuffed with a Wee Wanda cake, the crème puff filling now dotting his chin.

"Oh, here we go again—vampires can out-smell a werewolf anytime," Howard replied.

Wyatt let the conversation wash over him, his eyes darting every so often, searching for Nolan's silver pickup. He wondered if Jade was sweltering in the heat in Nolan's vehicle. Probably not. Nolan wouldn't have to worry about conserving gas. His dad would buy it for him.

"That was mine." Sean reached forward, trying to grab a powdered doughnut from Melvin's hand. Melvin shoved the rest into his mouth.

"Cut it out." Wyatt leaned over and punched his brother. "Look, I'll turn this sucker around and take you home—"

"No!" Melvin and Sean cried out in unison.

"Peace, bro." Sean made a *v* with his fingers.

"How seventies of you," Howard said, pushing his glasses up. His face was glazed with sweat. "It's so hot in here."

Melvin returned the peace sign and then flipped Sean the bird. Sean's retaliation was cut off as the car before them moved ahead a few feet. Wyatt turned the ignition on, lurching forward. The line started moving. They heard cheers from other cars around them. Melvin gave the thumbs-up signal to the car next to him.

The road split into six lanes with dozens of the new Monsterland staff waving flags, directing them to pull forward. A uniformed officer stepped into Wyatt's view, directing them to stop. He was wearing the black jumpsuit of Monsterland; his red badge had the logo with his name in the center. Wyatt could feel the excitement level in the car amp up. Sean sat on the edge of the seat, and Wyatt looked at him in the mirror. "Put your seatbelt back on."

"What?" he replied. "We're stopped."

Wyatt picked up his cell, threatening to call their mother. Sean ungraciously threw himself backward to put on his belt.

The officer peered into the back of the car, his flashlight illuminating the dark interior. Wyatt studied him with interest.

"We've set up a dumping station at the main gate. No food or beverages allowed," he informed them, looking into the car.

"I'm highly allergic and need specific food," Howard lied,

testing the officer.

"Sorry, son. We have a designated phone number where special meals can be ordered." He pushed up the visor of his hat. "You needed to call in advance, though. Too late for that. I know someone who'd want to buy your ticket."

"I'll suffer," Howard said dramatically.

The car inched forward, and the view was blocked by the row of tour buses in front of them. The vehicle before them turned left, and the boys sat in shocked awe as the vista opened. A massive concrete wall obliterated the horizon, giant iron gates separating them from the theme park.

"Entrance at oh twelve hundred," Melvin said in a clipped robotic voice.

"The gate!" Sean crowed, jumping like a wild man in his seat. His seatbelt was off again.

The entrance loomed before them. The first thing Wyatt noticed was the Monsterland logo, a large M in the center of vampire teeth. He looked up, spying iron letters barely visible in an arc overhead, the letters shaped with black metal. Wyatt stared at the gateway, his mouth dry. He had wanted so badly to go, all these months, plotting and planning a way to be able to attend, yet the sign pulled at a distant memory. The large lettering cast an imposing shadow. The iron gate was surrounded by twenty-foot-high, finely sloped concrete walls that made the place look like Hoover Dam.

Cut—it—out, Sean, or I'm calling Mom. You're not allergic to anything, Howard; and, Melvin, there's no such thing as 'oh twelve hundred.'"

"It's the coordinates."

"You're an idiot," Wyatt said with a laugh. Melvin was nothing if not entertaining.

"If you take me home, you're going to miss Jade." Sean pointed to the pickup truck pulling up in the next lane. Nolan had the window open and was arguing with the Monsterland police.

Wyatt craned his neck to see if he could get a glimpse of Jade. His heart started to beat faster; a telltale flush rose to paint his face when he spied her delicate profile. He leaned forward to get a better look at her.

"Forget it; she doesn't see you," Howard observed. "They're like the Gestapo," he added.

"The who?" Sean asked.

"The Nazis' special police."

"*Who's* like the Gestapo?"

"The Monsterland security. Did you hear that guy?"

"What's up with you, Howard Drucker? I thought you wanted to go." Wyatt turned, looking at his friend's pinched face.

"Yeah, that was before, this is now."

Melvin hooked his arm around the headrest. "What's that supposed to mean?"

Howard shrugged indifferently.

"Come on," Melvin said.

"In theory, it sounded like a very good idea. You know, seeing vampires, zombies, and werewolves in their natural habitat."

"So?"

"The point is, this," he gestured to the massive gates looming before them. "It seems unnatural. It feels—"

"What? Wrong? What else are they going to do with them? Kill them like in an old George Romero movie? This is so right," Melvin said. "They were dying in those detention camps."

"Containment camps," Howard corrected.

"Whatever." Melvin threw up his hands. "The hillbillies practically wiped out the werewolf colony once it was discovered. Vampires lived in fear, almost harried out of existence. Here they are protected. If they did that to the rhinos, maybe they wouldn't have become extinct."

"It's sterile, not real!" Howard was leaning over the front seat.

"What happened to you? You were so excited about it," Wyatt asked.

"This was all over the internet this morning." He typed something on his cell and then showed them the screen. It looked like a dilapidated portion of any American city. The image was filmed in a choppy fashion, bouncing around, going in and out of focus. The Werewolf River Run sign was in the viewfinder. Uniformed men, some with lab coats, entered the ride area. The camera panned out to view an artificial river with alligators rhythmically rising and falling in the water. There was a rustle and then shouts. A howl turned into a wail, and all four boys watched, their collective breaths held.

"Was that filmed inside Monsterland?"

"Shut up and listen. They're speaking English, so I guess it was right here."

"Who did it?"

Howard shrugged. *"America's Funniest Home Videos.* How the hell am I supposed to know? They didn't give any credits."

They clustered their heads together, fighting for space to see. Howard shoved the phone into Wyatt's hands so he could hold it up for them all.

The camera picked up a scuffle and then a muffled curse. An enormous dark animal tore from the brush, a gang of men following in hot pursuit. Its body was longer than a wolf, its hair a mix of black with gray highlights. It appeared to be about nine feet long. It growled, jumping high, and then, landing on all fours, it crouched low, snarling ominously. Its muscled shoulders bunched with raw power. Its mouth opened to reveal dripping yellow fangs that glistened in the light. Narrowing its golden eyes, it circled the area, and the men backed away warily. The paws were the size of dinner platters, and its broad chest heaved as it panted. Vincent Konrad was the tallest man in the group. He wore a white lab coat.

"A werewolf," Melvin whispered in wonder.

"Watch," Howard said.

The beast was overwhelmed by a Taser shot at him. It cried out in agony. Four goons jumped on its back. It was pummeled mercilessly with metal bats. In the background, the screams of a dozen beasts could be heard, but a row of men brandishing rifles held them in check. The animal was beaten, and, when it lay senseless on the floor, it was given one last kick.

The guard stood, wiping his hands. "Is it still breathing?" he asked, breathless from his exertion.

The doctor bent over to examine the creature. "Barely."

"Is that Vincent Konrad?" Sean tried to grab the cell phone.

"Shut up and watch!"

"Good. Feed it to the zombies. They like their meat alive." Vincent stood, wiping his hands on a proffered towel.

"Whoa, that's sick." Wyatt's eyes opened wide.

"I heard the whales took a worse beating at the aquarium," Melvin quipped.

"That couldn't have been Vincent —he wouldn't do that," Wyatt said with disbelief. He sat back, his stomach feeling unsettled, as if his world had suddenly tilted on its axis. Vincent Konrad was a man of honor, and that video had to be a mistake, he reasoned.

"Who are you?" Howard demanded. "That was murder, and, the last time I checked, murder was against the law." He fiddled with the white pocket protector, sliding out a pencil to look at its point.

"You are such a nerd," Melvin said, watching him.

Howard slid the pencil back hastily, making his nervous fingers relax in his lap.

"It's not murder if they aren't human." Melvin said.

"Who decides who is human?" Howard shouted back.

Melvin downed a can of Whisp in one gulp and belched in Howard's face.

The sign loomed above them. The car inched forward as if it were hooked on a tram ride. The back door was opened, and capable hands pulled out the cooler and bottled drinks. They were ordered out of the car. Two white-uniformed men appeared on either side with large vacuum hoses. They vacuumed the crumbs from the front of Melvin's shirt. He giggled as the suction pulled at his clothes.

"Hey, what's going on?" Wyatt asked. He noticed Nolan, Theo, Jade, and Keisha were also outside their vehicle. Jade's worried eyes found Wyatt's. Jade bit her bottom lip. Keisha waved her entrance ticket.

Wyatt pulled out his phone and started a text to Jade and then caught sight of Nolan and shoved his cell back in his pocket. What was he doing? *She has a boyfriend,* he reminded himself.

"We're supposed to be special guests," Keisha yelled at the lead guard.

"Yeah, join the crowd. Everybody has those today. You're all special," the guard retorted.

They were allowed back into the cars and told to follow the signage to the garages that rose out of the desert like a modernistic mountain.

"That wasn't so bad," Sean suggested.

"I don't know about this place," Howard replied.

"You're always the skeptic," Melvin said.

"So explain the video."

The ride to the garage was utterly silent. Wyatt glanced back in his rearview mirror and shifted uncomfortably in his seat, remembering why the sign unnerved him. It bore a striking resemblance to a picture he had seen in his history book. The words were in German and read *Arbeit Macht Frei—* Work Makes You Free. It was the entrance to the Auschwitz death camp.

Chapter 9

Billy's sharp eyes scanned the soldered joints holding the glass-covered dome together. He was in human form, as was the rest of his pack. The loincloths that had been given out earlier lay in a discarded heap where they had taken turns urinating on them, so they'd be unwearable.

This place was nothing better than a zoo. The collar on Billy's neck chafed his skin. He was rubbed raw by it; the green LED light was always on the edge of his peripheral vision, a constant reminder of his captivity.

Vincent Konrad made a mockery of science. He had no intention of finding a cure or studying the inhabitants, of that Billy was sure. The man was evil; his cold, obsidian eyes studied Billy as though he were nothing more than an insect under a microscope. They couldn't communicate with the other inmates of the theme park. If only they could reach out to them, they could band together to get out of here.

For all he knew, the vamps were happy with their confinement. Maybe they'd cut a better deal. Forget about the zombies; they were little better than a meal for his kind.

If only the vamps would respond to his calls. He had tried,

but they were cliquish, thought they were better than anyone else. Vamps cared for nothing except for their pleasure.

Vampires had passed for years living within society, on the fringe—they still managed to carve out a place for themselves, until Vincent saw fit to incorporate them into his obscene operation. They were invited in, not drugged and dragged in like he handled the werewolves. Werewolves had lived peacefully for years in the swamps until Vincent hunted them down to put them in his freak show.

Billy peered through the glass at the Vampire Village, trying to make contact with someone, anyone. He knew a vamp once; his name was Axel, of all things, infected when he was a roadie for one of the bands he followed.

They were a cautious group, those vamps, initiating only those who desired to be included. Sure, they made drones, people they fed off, taking blood. Those drones begged for it and then turned into groupies whose slavish devotion ended when the vamp stopped sucking their blood for a month straight. Nobody seemed too bothered by it except for the Bible-thumpers, but they balked at everything. Vampire numbers had dwindled as their popularity decreased. Even his buddy Axel disappeared one day.

Then Vincent came along, promising a safe home to what was left of the vampire population. They could have the run of the place, unlike the wolves, who he'd stuck in cages.

It's just that—Billy reasoned—*why didn't they realize they were making a pact with the devil?* If he imprisoned one group, another was just as endangered. If Vincent were to succeed, he needed the help of the vamps, 'cause everybody knew you couldn't reason with the zombies, poor souls. Once those suckers caught the virus, they declined until there was nothing left but an empty shell.

Billy growled deep in his throat, his sharp eyes scrutinizing the park. To the left, he saw a huge sign announcing wait times for the zombie suburbs. Vincent had no intention of creating a cure. *Why would he ruin his star attraction?* Vincent probably had plans to make more zombies. After all, he had several more of these theme parks premiering all over the world tonight.

Billy howled to his pack. He had spread his group to the four corners of their prison, getting familiar with their new territory.

Behind the theme park, he saw a line of rust-and-dun-colored mountains. They were far from the humid swamps of the south, but he had a rather sketchy idea of geography.

He barely remembered school or even his family. He had a new one now, and he had to protect his clan. Just over a ridge, he made out a snaking line of people waiting patiently to enter this strange land where he had been brought to live.

His fingers gripped the metal tightly, his jaw going slack. They were coming to see him, to point and study—and laugh. He jumped down, his heart racing.

It was dusk outside, but soon the artificial sky inside the dome would simulate the onset of evening allowing the bright full moon to assault both his and his friends' nervous systems. He knew their skin would stretch, their limbs would lengthen, and they would howl in pained agony. Hunger so great would turn them into eating machines, and they would attack anything in their paths.

He walked down a grassy trail, throwing himself onto a bed of moss. He was trapped in a controlled home where he would be the show. He understood now. This is why they had been taken from their homes. It was not to study them but to entertain bored school children looking for thrills.

Petey and Little John sniffed at the air, letting out a yelp of warning. They were coming back.

He had the rest of his group studying the routines of their keepers, checking for weakness in the security of the place. They had an army of guards, the same military types that had captured them late last year.

They spent a long time underground in a medical facility, being probed, and, in Todd's case, dissected to find out the reason they were half man, half beast. They had lost a few, allowed three new pack members in whose leader had been killed and skinned in the name of science.

The alarms rang, and Billy reluctantly rose, walking to his cell. He pulled at the collar on his neck, feeling the band pulse with the current that zapped him when he didn't obey. It wouldn't come off, this indestructible collar; there wasn't even a weak seam for him to wiggle. They had tried biting them off each other, only to be rewarded with a teeth-jarring zap that went straight to the middle of their heads. *Oh, the pain of that shock,* Billy remembered.

The door opened, and he crouched low to enter, holding on to the bars as they locked back in place. He exchanged a questioning glance with Petey, who nodded abruptly, letting him know he had some success.

The doors slammed shut, and he wondered why they were being locked up at this hour. Usually, they were allowed to run free all day. *Perhaps Vincent was coming.*

Vincent Konrad was a frequent visitor. Of course, Billy remained mum; they all had. None of them talked to humans; they wouldn't give anything away. Alone, they used nods, grunts, whines, and barks to communicate. It was enough.

He couldn't figure out Vincent's motive. *What did he want from them?* The doctor would come by and stand outside his pen for hours, locked in a silent duel, leaving Billy clueless to what the man's intent could be. *Was it all for science? Or a sadistic form of amusement?* Billy sensed it was something much more sinister than that, but he just couldn't put his finger on it.

Still, Vincent Konrad was not hostile. There was almost an indulgent air about him, as if Billy were his pet. Resentment roiled through Billy's body. The doctor's secretive smile infuriated him.

Billy was still in human form, scrabbling around in the dirt of his small cell, the domed ceiling muting all daylight. He knew it was nearing night; his internal clock told him so. He rolled on the floor of his pen: feces, chicken bones, and a mess of feathers on the filthy floor.

"What's the matter, Billy? Didn't your mother teach you manners? Look at this mess," the jailor taunted. "I guess she was too busy rutting with a wolf."

"You leave my mother alone!" Billy forced the words from his throat, feeling them scrape his rusty vocal cords like a file. The sentence came out garbled, barely intelligible, but he dragged the words from the recesses of his past to spit them out.

He screamed from the pain of his atrophied throat muscles and rammed against the gate. In truth, Billy barely remembered his mother. He had fled his home when he realized that he was not like his brothers. Billy was different, his strangeness causing them to keep a distance. He tried to fit in but knew instinctively he didn't belong.

It happened when night descended, and the moon gazed balefully down at him. His body would betray him, changing, shredding his clothes, forcing him to flee his home to search for food. The ravenous hunger would send him running, hunting, looking for a living thing to rip apart and devour. He would eat, bloodlust in his eyes, searching for and stealing chickens and dogs, until one day he found it was not enough.

When the moon disappeared, he felt himself return to his boyhood body to find the dismembered corpse of his neighbor spread about the greasy grass. He ran then, hiding during the day, foraging at night, howling at the moon, never resting until an answering cry told him he had found a home. There were seven others, all male, all the same.

They lived in the Everglades, away from humankind, living off the dense population of alligators—until Vincent Konrad had destroyed their peace.

"You filthy animal." The zookeeper yanked on a four-inch-wide hose, his face smiling evilly. "Got to get cleaned up. Company's coming."

Billy cringed as the nozzle jerked in the keeper's hands, spraying his pen with hurricane-force jets of water. He folded up, his naked body beaten by the cold liquid. It forced him into a corner, his feet slipping on the slimy, muddy floor. His unkempt hair lay coldly on his back in long rattails. The knobs of his spine rubbed the brick in the back of his pen, scraping it raw.

He surged forward, hitting the chain link fence so that it bowed outward, and he had the satisfaction of smacking against his jailor. His hands slid through the meal slot to grip the worker by his neck. Billy shook him like a rag doll. He snarled a smile at the satisfying *thunk* when the keeper fell on his backside. All the inmates laughed and then started their howling. Burning needles hit him on his hairy, naked chest when the guard tased him. Billy collapsed, breathlessly keeping his hands underneath him.

"I told you not to get too close!" a co-worker yelled as he pulled the guard to his feet. "You can't taunt them. You've been warned."

"Yeah, yeah. What are you going to do, replace me? Nobody wants to work in this stink hole," he grumbled. They left the room.

"You okay, Billy?" Petcy growled.

"Never better," Billy said, holding up a flat, plastic card. It was the passkey to all the cells.

Chapter 10

Carter leaned against the wall, his eyes scanning the growing crowd of dignitaries invited to the grand opening. Danny Jessup, his boss and chief of police, walked past him, pausing to take a sip from his ever-present coffee cup. He exchanged a look over the rim, catching Carter's shrug. Carter's phone vibrated with a message. He pulled it out, noting that Wyatt informed him he'd just arrived.

Carter texted back, "Can't now—on duty. Meet you later."

The press walked around, getting interviews from the guests. The air buzzed with excitement. Carter laughed. *It was like the friggin' Oscars,* he snorted to himself.

Jessup's deep-set eyes watched him intently. He was just past forty, and his love of burritos showed on his waistline. He hitched his pants and nodded. "Kids?"

"Yep. They've arrived. Yours?"

Jessup shook his head. "Nope. Told them I didn't want them here. Don't want distractions."

Carter nodded. "Mine got special invitations."

"You could have said no."

Carter cocked his head. "What, and be the evil stepfather? No thanks. I'm still working on getting them to play ball with me." He looked at the coffee cup. "I thought we weren't allowed food or beverages in the park."

"We *are* considered to be in a safe zone," Jessup said with a smirk.

"Duly noted," Carter stated, as if that was all that had to be said. They had worked together for close to fifteen years and could practically read each other's thoughts. "Something doesn't feel right."

"Too many important people here. I heard the ambassadors from both Germany and Russia just landed," Jessup said, looking at his watch. "Not to mention the president, a clutch of senators, and a bunch of militaries."

Carter nodded to a brace of suited men obviously in the Secret Service. "They've brought their own guns."

"Not enough for my taste. The way I see it, we're outnumbered at least a hundred to one."

"That only counts if this thing goes south," Carter said. "Konrad keeps assuring everybody he's got it under control. The inhabitants are heavily sedated."

"I'm not comfortable with it." Jessup threw his cup into a garbage can.

"I read the playbook. Monsterland has protocols in place. The wolves are behind impenetrable glass, they keep the vampires sated with blood, and the zombies are in a walled-off village. Visitors wear special suits."

"It seems Dr. Konrad thought of everything," Jessup said.

"Yeah," Carter laughed. "And they said the *Titanic* wouldn't sink either." There was a bite of sarcasm in Carter's voice. "What could possibly go wrong? Have you talked to them?" He gestured to the Secret Service.

Jessup inclined his head. "Seems they dance to their own drum. They don't want to expose any plans on how they protect the president. We appear to be on our own."

"Sometimes it's better that way. I still don't like it," Carter said with a shake of his head.

"What, in particular, is bothering you?" Jessup asked.

"Well, start with the fact that we are surrounded by a hostile population...."

"He seems to be well organized. He has security in place. You saw the wall of guns." They had been given a tour of the park earlier and shown a room with mounted shotguns. The ammo shells were loaded with silver shot.

Carter shook his head. "I don't understand why he keeps his arsenal under lock and key."

"He explained it all." Jessup shrugged. "The park is filled with silver axes behind glass doors every ten feet, for emergency use. The silver works on all three groups, the axe on anybody. He didn't want armed guards in the park. I get that. The whole place is under surveillance. He looks like he's got a good security team here. Created a lot of jobs."

Carter laughed. "Yeah. They're an odd bunch."

"What do you mean?"

"Just a feeling. I can't quite put my finger on it, Dan. I don't know. It's just a feeling."

"Well." Jessup put his hand on Carter's shoulder. "Keep your feelings to yourself."

Chapter 11

Zombieville was set up like a bizarre television or movie set, with tree-lined streets and pastel-colored bi-level homes. They could have been in a small suburban town anywhere in the States.

Maintenance people patrolled alongside guards dressed in metal armor, not unlike chain mail. This prevented the zombies from biting and infecting them. It was only through the exchange of body fluids that the disease traveled. Their faces covered, they walked through the byways, cleaning blood and guts from the pristine streets.

There were a total of twenty homes, each filled to capacity with pus-covered, rotted wrecks of humanity that dozed in a drugged stupor all day, roused by their keepers with the tantalizing smell of meat when the sun slipped behind the mountains. They would wake each other, moaning with desperation to get to the food, climbing over each other to find a way out of their four-walled confines to the large tube that brought the food into the development.

They didn't talk to each other; their brains had lost the ability to communicate anything other than the driving need to consume flesh. They burst out of the door, staggering across the manicured lawns, their arms stretched out before them to feel what they could find and feed the voracious hunger keeping them alive.

He couldn't believe he'd ended up here. He had to get out. Some remnant of his mind told him he needed to feel fresh air. Vincent had put him here, of that he was sure. He had gone into the danger zone for him, for Vincent. He returned to find himself changing within a few hours of being infected.

At first, his skin turned putty-like, its color the pale green of celery. His bones became brittle, and his hair fell out in clumps. *Where was the hospital,* he wondered? Vincent was supposed to take care of him. They had a deal. He had a deal!

Instead, he was shipped off to an internment camp in the remotest part of Montana. Now this—the man scanned the wreckage of humanity lying in catatonic oblivion.

A bell sounded. The call to food. He knew where he was —it wasn't an invitation to food. It was the call to make Vincent richer and even more powerful than he ever was. Not him. He was a Rhodes scholar once. He graduated at the top of his class. He was a family man—well, he was once.

He stood, pushing a woman out of the way, stepping on her leg, not caring when he heard her femur break. Side-tracked, he spun, watching her fold on her unsteady leg.

She sank to the floor, her hand clasping her head. He smelled the blood of her wound as it seeped from her crushed leg onto the floor.

They were on her in a minute—the room filled with the sound of her flesh being torn from her bones, the splatter of her body fluids as they hit the concrete floor.

The man turned back, grabbing her wrist in his hand. He pulled, watching in fascination as it detached from her body, the rubbery tendons glistening in the light. He put it to his lips and ate.

Chapter 12

They parked the car on the ninth level, and Howard Drucker promised to remember it because it reminded him of the ninth circle of hell from Dante's *Inferno*, which he had just read for AP English.

There was the ever-present sound of water dripping, creating an eerie mood. The crowd was strangely subdued. They met up with Nolan and the others at the elevator. They piled in like sardines in a can, and when the pneumatic doors closed, Wyatt was surprised to feel his brother stand very close to him.

The doors opened to bright floodlights turning night into day, a concrete path with green areas on either side.

A red carpet had been spread; all the major television networks were there. Giant strobe lights crisscrossed in the sky, creating white beams that seemed to go to the heavens. Beautiful reporters in long gowns talked into bejeweled mics to actors and actresses, all holding tickets. Some held parchments, and others held silver strips like the ones Vincent had given Nolan. Everybody was tense with anticipation, thrilled to be included in this exclusive activity.

The noise level was high, and flash bulbs burned Wyatt's retinas, but he and his group were largely overlooked because of all the talent that arrived.

Water gushed from a waterfall, and birds screeched from the swaying palm trees. Wyatt's eyes searched for the familiar khaki-colored uniform of his stepfather. He saw, instead, a sea of Monsterland employees dressed in black jumpsuits.

"This is creepy," Wyatt told his brother in a hushed whisper.

"You were expecting Knott's Berry Farm?" Wyatt heard Howard Drucker say from behind.

Melvin walked briskly before them, taking in the lush scenery. Wyatt felt a person near his other side and smiled when he realized Jade had come up close to him. She returned his greeting, her eyes softening. They walked close together, squeezed by the packed crowd. The air charged between them, and Wyatt felt his heart beat a bit faster. Nolan stood slightly behind her. He gave Wyatt a dirty look and then grabbed Jade's hand, pulling her to walk next to him.

Wyatt turned around, looking for Howard Drucker, and didn't see him through the crowd. His eyes met Keisha's, who brightened and motioned that Howard was now beside her. Wyatt recognized the top of his friend's head.

They shuffled en masse along the winding path that opened to a vast plaza with three life-sized statues of monsters on a grassy knoll in the center.

The noise level increased as they got closer, and voices meshed together until they seemed like a giant beehive of people. At the end of the walkway, they unwound from the tight ball they had become. There was a bronze plaque and a bust of Vincent Konrad next to it.

People milled around the plaque. Wyatt pushed through to read the contents.

"Monsterland was created with the sole intent of introducing the habitat of those unfortunate creatures to create a better understanding of the species with which we share our world. Dr. Vincent Konrad is working hand-in-hand with the government to foster tolerance and keep our different environments from colliding," Sean read aloud. There was applause and scattered chatter.

Three helicopters rose from the theme park, creating black outlines against the stars. Their rotors whipped the trees to life, and the crowd instinctively ducked as the choppers hovered and then headed east toward the airport.

With grinding gears, a row of solid iron doors slid open, revealing murky walkways. Attendants dressed in crisp green uniforms stood like silent sentinels at each portal, their faces impassive. Melvin raced ahead to be the first one in the park.

People surged forward like cattle, dividing into small groups to enter the turnstiles one by one. Wyatt gripped his brother's sleeve, pushing him in front where he could keep his eye on him. He saw Nolan holding Jade possessively by the hand as they went through the entrance to his right.

Wyatt pulled his parchment from his back pocket where it had been folded into a neat square. He handed the girl his invitation, which she examined. She searched his face to see if she could recognize him as someone special. She gave up with an embarrassed shrug and told him to keep the parchment as a souvenir. She handed him a map of the park and directed him to an escalator where he saw Melvin halfway to the top. Wyatt stuffed the map in his back pocket.

Wyatt saw Nolan go to another doorway. The jock looked at him with an exaggerated shrug, Wyatt shrugged back. He noticed Jade was close to the quarterback's hulking side. Wyatt turned to the attendant and asked, "My friends, can they join us here?"

"No," she said. "Dr. Konrad is waiting to take you on a private behind-the-scenes tour. You can catch up with them later."

"Come on," Melvin shouted, waving wildly from the top of the escalator. "Let's go!"

Wyatt followed his brother toward the steep moving stairs, his eyes searching and finding Jade as she disappeared through a portal. He saw Howard walking slightly behind Keisha.

"Howard Drucker!" he shouted. "You're supposed to be over here!"

Keisha looked up. She was holding onto Howard by the back of his shirt. Howard smiled sheepishly and winked.

"Well, that's one way to get him to take her on a date," Melvin observed.

"He thinks he's not good enough for her," Wyatt answered.

"He's not, but it looks like it doesn't matter," Sean laughed.

"She's aggressive; I'll give her that. What did Vincent call her, Diana the Huntress?" Melvin asked.

"Looks like she finally got her prey," Sean added. "But it should be the other way around. Howard Drucker should be the hunter."

"Howard Drucker wouldn't know how to hunt, even if a deer landed in his lap and said, 'Take me,'" Wyatt said with a chuckle.

"And you would?" Melvin asked him.

Wyatt didn't answer. Melvin was already getting on his nerves, and they hadn't even gone inside yet. He wished Howard had stayed with him. Wyatt watched mutely as Keisha and Howard were dragged through the entrance, Theo trailing behind them, to be swallowed by the crowd. He didn't know why, but he felt uneasy as their heads disappeared.

The escalator rounded the top and Wyatt stepped on the backs of his brother's feet as they were pushed onto the mezzanine. Sean turned, yelling, "Hey!" He stumbled ahead, his sneaker half off his right foot.

They were in a glass-enclosed visitors center. It spanned the entire left side and contained the control center that ran Monsterland.

They were halted by an attendant who slapped bracelets around their wrists. Wyatt fingered the material, but couldn't find a beginning or end to the tag. It was locked securely on his arm. He looked up at the attendant who smiled. "It indicates you are one of the chosen guests. You won't have to wait on long lines."

Wyatt nodded with understanding, but he was feeling trapped in the crowd. A woman with a mic approached him, her cameraman trailing behind.

"And you are ...?" She held out the mic.

"Wyatt Baldwin."

"Any relation to Alec?" She craned her neck hoping to catch sight of him.

Wyatt shook his head. "Sorry, nope. I mean, no relation."

"How'd you get to VIP?" she asked, looking at the three of them. "What, did you win the tickets in a raffle?"

Wyatt backed away from her. She was a predator, making him feel tiny and exposed.

"Hey, kid ... Baldwin boy. I have a question," she called out to him.

"Go talk to a politician," Melvin yelled over his shoulder as they pressed through the groups of people.

There were hundreds of people in business suits milling throughout the reception area. They pushed into the center and stopped. Wyatt stared, his mouth open. He saw the governor, two state senators, and the Speaker of the House all in one cluster, surrounded by men in dark glasses.

He noticed a few of his stepfather's colleagues in their beige uniforms skirting the mob of people. His eyes scanned the crowd for Carter. He wanted to talk to him—*well, not really.* He wanted to see him, just for a second. He knew he would feel more settled if he did.

Right now, his insides buzzed with a weird sense of nervous anticipation, as if he were riding to the top of a rollercoaster but wasn't prepared for the drop. He knew it was coming but had no idea when—or how frightening. His stomach tightened into a knot, and his skin was sensitive so that when he brushed against Sean, he jumped. Sean pushed him with a nervous snort.

Wyatt saw Vincent then, glad-handing the crowd. Above them, screens were set up, each displaying different Monsterland openings all over the world. Vincent Konrad was looking at the monitors, laughing at the antics of politicians and celebrities at each of the seven parks worldwide. Every major leader was there. No one wanted to miss being invited to the biggest event since the biblical flood. Vincent walked around like a candidate running for office, a huge smile pasted on his face.

Wyatt studied the doctor, shaking his head. *This man couldn't have killed that wolf, wouldn't have fed it to the zombies. He was a humanitarian. It had to be actors.* It went against everything Vincent stood for.

There were representatives from all arms of the military— generals, admirals, and foreign dignitaries. Women in Monsterland jumpsuits walked around with black trays full of cocktails and small appetizers. Sean reached forward, snagging a handful of pigs in blankets, stuffing them into his mouth.

"Sean," Wyatt admonished.

"What, they're free, and we're guests." Sean lurched to the right. "Melvin!" he called as he ran to Wyatt's buddy, who had a martini in each hand. "Give me one!"

"Melvin, what are you doing?" Wyatt said, then added, "If you give my brother a drink, you're dead."

Melvin grinned, downing one martini, placing the empty glass on a table. He slurped the other drink, his eyes half-closed in ecstasy. He rushed to the other side of the room.

Wyatt rolled his eyes and then squeezed through the crowd, listening to the conversations, mostly business. He reached Melvin, who was now leaning casually against the wall.

"You're going to get us thrown out of here," Wyatt told Melvin.

"Vincent Konrad needs us more than we need him," Melvin responded, spitting as he spoke.

Sean raced over, his face flushed with excitement. "There's McAdams." Sean pointed to the president. Wyatt pulled him back, forcing them to melt into the crowd. "What? Cut it out. You're just like Mom."

Wyatt took in Melvin's flushed face. "You look drunk."

"Just happy. I can handle it."

"I don't want to have to clean up your vomit."

"You sound like your mom. Relax, Wyatt. Where's Howard Drucker?"

Wyatt peered through a thick glass wall, pointing to a crowded entrance. "He got swept away with Keisha. He never made it up here." He texted Howard, but the message wouldn't go through.

"Well, I'm bored. Let's go," Sean said.

"I want to hear the president's speech," Wyatt said.

"Look, I'm here for fun, not a history lesson. I'm going, with or without you."

The president mounted the mezzanine, the crowd parting in awe. Vincent Konrad came forward, a broad smile on his face. He held out welcoming arms to the leader of the free world, who walked right into the mogul's embrace. They shook hands warmly, and Vincent put his arm around McAdam's back.

Wyatt studied him for a minute. He had taken a course last year on the body language of diplomacy. The doctor had his arm around the president's shoulders and was declaring himself the dominant man in the room, the more powerful person.

Sound receded for Wyatt; he cocked his head, staring at them. Vincent's eyes scanned the room, stopping to rest on him. The black eyes locked on Wyatt like the dual bores of a rifle. Wyatt shivered but held the gaze. Vincent's thin lips widened into a mirthless smile that seemed to be directed solely to Wyatt, hitting him like an invisible force field. Vincent nodded once. Wyatt felt his scalp tighten.

The room felt small, too hot. The doctor's face seemed unfamiliar, as if the stark light revealed a new person. Wyatt didn't want to hear anything this person had to say. He wanted to leave. "Let's go." He turned toward the upper entrance.

"I thought you wanted to hear the president's speech."

"I changed my mind," Wyatt said, his voice low. He briefly considered leaving the park. Jade was with Nolan, and he was stuck with his brother. Melvin was acting odd, and Howard was missing. This was not what he expected.

He looked over the railing at the vast expanse of Monsterland. The noise of the eager crowd was muffled through the thick glass. LED screens displayed wait times for various attractions. *Zombies*, he thought. When would he ever get this chance again? If nothing else, he wanted to see them up close.

For years, all things zombie had consumed him. He had read everything he could get his hands on. He couldn't explain his fascination; he could talk about them for hours. Lately, though, they didn't seem as appealing as they used to.

Jade, on the other hand, was much more appealing. It had first occurred to him that zombies weren't exactly scintillating conversation when he had watched Jade's eyes glaze over when they did the report together this past semester. He didn't mind when she turned the conversation to something else. Not that he could remember that discussion either. It seemed all he could concentrate on were her ice-blue eyes and creamy skin.

If only he could tell if Jade was really interested in him. Carter told him to ask her out—she wasn't engaged, didn't wear Nolan's ring or anything.

In fact, Keisha whispered that Jade wasn't too crazy about Nolan and had talked about backing out of her prom date with him. Nolan was leaving this fall, got a full football scholarship to Idaho State. Jade was going to nursing school right here in Copper Valley. She was staying home, like him. Maybe, she'd go to the movies. *Maybe not.* He frowned. He searched for her face in the crowd but asked his companions absently, "You want to do the behind-the-scenes tour?"

Melvin looked longingly through the glass observation windows at the park spread below them. "Hell, no."

"Me neither," Sean agreed.

"Let's see what we came for." Wyatt nodded. He turned to scan the room once more, catching sight of his stepfather. Carter gave him a wry smile. Wyatt waved his hand in a friendly salute and turned with his friends to the large pneumatic doors guarded by two men in black uniforms.

"If you leave this way, there's no way back," one of them said ominously.

Wyatt gulped.

"The park has exits." Melvin walked up to one of them, his face close to the guard.

He nodded. "Yes, but once you leave these doors, you can't return this way."

"Let's go," Sean said urgently.

The guard pressed a combination of numbers into a keypad, and the doors opened, revealing a pitch-black tunnel.

"It's dark in there," Wyatt said, peering into the blackness. "Like a vacuum."

"It lights up automatically overhead as you walk through. Go on." He gestured to the passageway. "I can't keep this open long."

They ran into the dark, tube-like structure that lit the spot they were in as they traveled through it, their feet echoing in the empty chamber. Wyatt paused for a second, looking at where they came from, the tunnel lights extinguishing so that the way back was as dark as the sky. He shook as if chilled.

"This place is so cool!" Sean said, his voice echoing in the dimly lit corridor. "What's wrong with you? Come on, look." He pointed to the dark alley. "There's no going back."

"Yeah," Wyatt agreed. He looked at the lights before him and the darkness behind him. His brother was right. There was no going back.

Chapter 13

Vincent Konrad was in his element, he observed, as the older man walked through the groups, shaking hands, smiling his toady smile. Carter leaned forward, his hands fisted on his hips, his gun reassuringly belted to his side, another, snug in his ankle holster.

His eyes began to circle the room, his ears alert to the steady hum of conversation. He had felt the doctor's presence before he saw him.

"Officer White," the doctor read off his badge. He didn't offer his hand. "Are you enjoying the park?"

"I'm here to work." Carter dragged his gaze from a group of politicians to meet Vincent's face. "I'm not here for enjoyment."

"All work and no play will make you a dull boy," Vincent said with a laugh.

Carter shrugged indifferently. "I've been called worse."

"You refused our complimentary tickets for your family."

"My sons are here."

"I don't remember the White family on the guest list."

Carter shifted his weight. "My stepsons are named Baldwin. You gave Wyatt Baldwin tickets at Instaburger."

"Ah!" Vincent threw back his head. "A delightful young man. He did you proud that day. He is somewhat familiar to me." He studied Carter's face with a calm smile. Carter felt those black orbs search him so intently; he felt like his own eyes were being sucked from their sockets.

Carter looked away. He asked, "Do you know everybody who enters your park?"

"I make it my business to know everything and everybody that touches my enterprises. That's the secret to my success." Vincent placed a heavy hand on Carter's shoulder. Carter couldn't help but wince at the contact. "Suppose you lead the way into these rooms so that I can begin my tour, Officer White. Maybe I can change your mind about my venture."

Carter turned. "How do you know how I feel about your … venture?"

He felt the hard scrutiny of the older man's gaze. The black eyes studied him intently, and, for a minute, the silence was so thick it felt tangible. Carter felt the urge to shift but refused to be the first to give in. He returned Vincent's stare, his cheek taut with the effort.

Vincent broke the hold first, laughing. "I told you, Officer White. I make it my business to know. Please lead the guests to the control center."

The group of dignitaries followed both Carter and Vincent through the halls, the sounds of the excited crowd filling the canned interior. Vincent approached a double door with a keypad on the side. Jessup brought up the rear.

Carter leaned against the wall as Vincent punched in the numbers. Carter nonchalantly observed and couldn't explain why it seemed important to him to watch. *Five-eight-forty-five-oh-five,* he repeated in his head. Vincent watched him silently and then covered the keypad for the last number. He punched it with a flourish. The doors opened with an efficient *whoosh.*

They passed the weapons room, the doctor proudly pointing to rows and rows of twelve-gauge shotguns, each with a pouch of shiny shotgun shells the size of his thumb. Carter nodded appreciatively. *They would stop a werewolf, vampire, or zombie in their tracks,* he thought with satisfaction.

A diplomat took out a cell phone to take some video. He looked at Vincent, with a question in his eyes.

"Do you mind if I shoot this?"

"Be my guest. All of you." Vincent gestured broadly.

They all withdrew their cell phones and started taking pictures.

"Impressive firepower. I bet it would take down an elephant, rhino, or hippo as well," President McAdams added with a smile.

"Seems incongruous to have guns in a family theme park," the ambassador from Germany grumbled.

A few people murmured, the crowd shuffling uncomfortably.

"Welcome to the twenty-first century!" Vincent shouted with pride, ignoring the observation.

The doctor led them into a large facility lined with five rows of computer consoles. Uniformed techs sat absorbed at each screen.

Vincent walked briskly ahead, waving the president and his entourage forward. Carter lagged behind, and his group took positions in the back of the room, silent guards lining the curved wall with quiet observation.

The entire facing wall was a collection of hundreds of screens that changed with the rapidity of a blink. Naked men in pens, a dining area filled with Gothically dressed vampires, their pale faces large on the monitor. There were various shots of the park, close-ups of workers, guests, and monsters.

Carter heard scattered laughter. His attention was drawn to a screen which displayed a hunchback cavorting like a circus clown. Vampire Village loomed behind the disfigured creature.

The hunchback was surrounded by a circle of guests poking him with souvenir axes that were already being purchased in the stores. He was an ugly little man, dressed as a medieval jester.

The giant hump looked like an exaggeration. *That can't be real,* Carter snorted.

Another screen showed an infirmary with doctors in lab coats treating ailing inhabitants of the park. One room had rows of vampires having blood drawn.

President McAdams called out. "Are they giving or getting transfusions, Vincent?"

"Neither, Mr. President. We are taking their blood to study it." Vincent warmed to his subject. "Imagine, if you will, if we could isolate the enzyme in a vampire's blood and use it to tame a wild population."

"A wild population of what?" the Russian ambassador asked, his face alert.

"Why, of revolutionaries and malcontents. Think, gentlemen—war will be obsolete."

The room buzzed as some people debated the statement.

A general walked forward, considering the screen showing a vampire calmly having his blood withdrawn. "Sometimes being a revolutionary is not a bad thing, Dr. Konrad. Let's not forget our great country was founded by revolutionaries."

"The U.S. government is a democracy and would never turn against its people," Vincent retorted.

"Governments don't turn on the people; corrupt politicians do," the general said gruffly.

"Come now, General Anthony, is it?" Vincent asked. "We are talking about Vincent Konrad and the United States of America. We are all perfectly safe."

President McAdams walked over and pulled the general aside. They spoke, their faces serious. There appeared to be a disagreement, but the general was discreetly yet firmly disciplined.

Carter watched the exchange with fascination. Most people were absorbed with the many screens. There was a gasp, and a tremor seemed to travel through the group.

Carter's eyes were drawn to a monitor showing a deserted suburban street filled with picturesque split-level homes. The room grew silent as the guests turned their attention to the image of a house that turned into an interior shot. There was a collective inhale, followed by uncomfortable rumblings.

On the monitor, a mass of squirming people fought over something on the floor. The camera closed in on the back of one man's head. He turned, his eyes blank, his hand holding the disconnected limb of another, his mouth chewing rhythmically on fingers. No matter how many times Carter had seen situations like this on the news, it turned his stomach.

The room erupted with sounds of disgust.

Vincent snapped at one of his employees, and the scene changed to the main street of his park. President McAdams looked around, urging his team to be quiet with a stern look.

"Not a pleasant sight, ladies and gentlemen, but a stark reminder of what we are trying to accomplish here today," Vincent began. He had their attention now. "Monsterland was created with the help of President McAdams and his administration to prevent the spread of the virus, as well as to protect the entire population of the United States. Other countries have joined our grand plan to eliminate this scourge to society by following America's example." The room quieted as the guests listened with rapt interest. "By nature, we are curious creatures. I used my natural interest to discover werewolves. Using my resources, I captured them all and brought them to the various parks to prevent them from rampaging through our communities."

Carter smirked. He hadn't heard of any rampaging werewolves. Apparently, they had been in the Everglades for eons and had lived unnoticed by the rest of society. *Lie one,* he began his count.

Vincent continued. "Vampires have lived among us, on the fringe of society, for a long time, but their disregard for our values has made them a menace as well as a nuisance. Their wholesale thirst to corrupt our youth had to be stopped and stopped fast. No country is safe from those vermin."

Carter caught Jessup's face and rolled his eyes. Vamps had lived peacefully among the population for years. *They didn't bother us, and we didn't disturb them,* he thought. *Lie two.* They were dying out now, having trouble adding to their numbers. It was against the law to make someone a vampire, the punishment swift and terrible. Only the occasional disenfranchised teenagers found themselves sucking blood, but, generally, it had been brought under control years ago.

While they were known to prey on people intent to join their ranks, usually these victims were turned into drones and released when the blood drawing stopped. Carter shook his head. If you didn't give them an excuse to find a disengaged person, they eventually moved on elsewhere. Except for Melvin's mother, Carter couldn't think of another person he knew who had joined them. She ended up in Antarctica anyway.

"That brings us to the zombies."

"The *vitality-challenged,*" President McAdams corrected. "We don't like the other term."

"Of course." Vincent smiled. "The *vitality-challenged* presented a significant, expensive burden to the country as well as the world."

"We are working on a cure," the president said to the room at large, his hands outstretched with assurance.

"Indeed, we are," the doctor took over. "Having them here kills two birds with one stone. You see"—he directed this to the Russian diplomats "—making them available in a safe environment is better for the entire population. Now people can see them safely. Even though their camps were high in the mountains, pesky interlopers would go there to investigate and, sadly, were infected, putting more people at risk. Here," he said, pointing to a monitor, "we wear protective suits. We can study them, and people can see them without running the risk of bringing the infection home."

Murmurs of approval circulated through the crowd. Carter grudgingly admitted that Vincent trumped him there. He couldn't find fault with his logic—except he disapproved of making a freak show of people who were ill. Still, somehow it did feel like exploitation of the helpless. He couldn't approve any of it.

The screens filled with excited crowds clamoring to gain entrance.

Vincent gestured to the eager faces. "You see, ladies and gentlemen, with the help of all the governments of multiple nations, we have eliminated the danger, created a place to study, and alleviated the suffering of these beasts, and, perhaps —" he paused for effect "—we might even find that cure."

The room broke out with sounds of hearty applause. President McAdams came forward, a warm smile on his face, to shake Vincent's hand. "The people of the United States trust both their government and Dr. Vincent Konrad."

The Russian ambassador moved forward to join the two men, "I want to add that our government and the people of Russia support this plan."

Carter White exchanged a glance with Jessup. He didn't vote for this president, and he sure as hell didn't trust Vincent Konrad. "I thought we had a measure of freedom of choice in our country's decisions?" Carter said out the side of his mouth to his friend. "What happened to the rest of Congress?"

"Majority rules?" Jessup shrugged.

"What majority?" Carter asked.

The president continued, "The government stands behind Vincent Konrad and Monsterland as a window to the future, to preserve and protect the good people of these United States and the world."

This time the room erupted with cheers. Vincent leaned forward to whisper something into the president's ear. They shared a secret smile.

Carter turned to Jessup. "I'll bet you a week's salary that he's not sharing campaign tips."

Jessup nodded grimly. They both watched Vincent escort the president and the Russian ambassador out of the room.

Chapter 14

Their feet echoed in the tunnel. They ran faster, Melvin and Sean laughing nervously. The dark passageway seemed to go on forever. Wyatt eyed several doors built into the wall, small lit signs above, designating them as Staff Only. There were no doorknobs, he noted, simply a small red light with a keypad next to each of the almost-invisible doors.

The tunnel abruptly ended, opening to a windowless platform suspended over the park. Monsterland was spread below them in all its drab and dingy glory, a marvel of every nightmare a person could imagine.

Wyatt leaned over the railing, and the impact of the size of the park hit him. It was the biggest thing he'd ever seen.

"This is incredible," Melvin screamed with excitement.

Below them, an enormous wrought iron sign welcomed the guests to the old town square, a parody of Main Street, USA.

"*Monsterland—Enter at Your Own Risk.*" Sean read the tortured metal letters. He turned to Wyatt. "I love it here. This place kills me."

Melvin howled with laughter, repeating, "This place kills me. You are too funny, dude."

Wyatt didn't answer; he was busy taking in the recreated city. Instead of pastel buildings made with solid red bricks like in many of the theme parks of his youth, Monsterland was filled with dilapidated warehouses covered with graffiti. Desolate storefronts and dark alleyways with overflowing trash cans dotted the streets. A mist rose off the stained cobblestones. Many of the windows sported giant spider webs of cracked glass; doors hung drunkenly, the rooflines appeared uneven and patched. Here and there, the streets showed chalk outlines, as if police were examining multiple murders and had abandoned them mid-investigation.

It was as lonely and bleak as the end of the world.

The village was divided into three paths, each labeled with an imaginative sign.

"Blood Boulevard." Sean pointed to the first one, shouting out the name with glee.

Wyatt's eyes found the sign Plague Path. He knew instinctively where that would end. It had to be the road to Zombieville. He looked down at the map to confirm the information.

An opaque glass dome loomed over one of the attractions. Wyatt wasn't sure which one it covered until he saw part of the sign made from hewn timber. Even though he couldn't read the words to the attraction, he guessed it was the Werewolf River Run. *It doesn't take an Einstein to figure it out,* he thought. After all, it was located at the end of the street called Werewolf Way.

Huge blowers kept the air circulating in the heat, leaving the temperature at a steady seventy-five degrees. Wyatt surmised that it kept the flesh and blood in the attractions from rotting quickly in the desert heat. Antique street lamps gave off weak puddles of light, despite the giant hidden floodlights overhead. The halogen lights bathed the entire park in a surreal tone. Still, a miasma hung over the area like an extra purple layer of atmosphere.

Melvin took out his cell to make a video of the teeming crowd. He saw that Sean was busy recording as well. Piped-in music played on an audio system, sounding like soothing white noise. *A strange choice,* Wyatt thought. *Why weren't they playing rock music to amp up the ambiance?*

He held onto the side of the balcony to peer at the mass of patrons moving like a swollen river. The babble of hundreds of excited voices rose up and would have drowned out the music anyway, Wyatt realized.

"Look!" Sean pointed at vendors in garish costumes walking the streets with black and red balloons shaped like droplets of blood. There were kiosks with masks, toy weapons, T-shirts, but not a single cart with food. Wyatt saw that the streets were not desolate as he thought, but filled with ubiquitous, small boutique stores stocked with more products to purchase. A colossal, dark glass wall lined one whole side. It read "Commissary." Wyatt knew it opened in intervals, so people could go in to eat. It was sealed after it filled so that odors couldn't get out. No food was permitted in the park. The "acts" were fed regulated food and not allowed anything else.

His phone pinged with several messages. He looked at them. Jade asked for them to join their group on the line at the Werewolf River Run. Her text complained that they had a two-hour wait. Howard Drucker still hadn't told him where he was.

"The Werewolf River Run," Melvin said reverently, his eyes on the massive dome.

"I want to do Zombieville, right, Wy? Don't you want to see the zombies first?"

Wyatt gripped the railing, feeling small, insignificant next to the vastness of the park. *How had they built this so quickly and without anyone realizing the scope of the whole thing?* He ran to the other side of the balcony.

Squeezed into the northwest quadrant, Wyatt saw the outline of Vincent's haunted hotel, a resort that hadn't been finished in time for the opening. It was an old Victorian mansion on top of a hill with four copper turrets surrounded by an ornate black metal fence that glistened in the moonlight. Vincent's flag, a black pennant with the red Monsterland logo, flew from the tallest tower. He could see construction vehicles parked around the fenced off property.

He had read an article about a cave attraction that was due to open with Phase 2 next spring. It was said to run underneath the entire theme park with an underground roller coaster. Wyatt could only imagine what monsters Vincent had up his sleeve for that one.

Wyatt's phone buzzed again. This time Jade texted a message saying Nolan was looking for him. He stared down at the swirling mass of people and realized he'd never be able to find anyone. He sent a mass text to all his friends to look for the mezzanine.

Wyatt searched the park grounds. The people swarmed the broken cobbled streets. He noticed long lines at every attraction that spilled out into the Town Square. Some queues seemed to stretch all the way into the recesses of the park. He squinted, trying to find Nolan in the throngs of people. Nolan emerged from the crowd, jogging over toward the balcony. His face was red, and he was breathless.

"Come on down; we've been waiting for you!" he shouted. "Didn't you get our text?"

"Where's everybody?" asked Wyatt.

Nolan shrugged. "Who cares? Jade and I are in the queue for the Werewolf River Run. You can use that special pass to get us in the VIP line."

Wyatt fiddled with the black rubber band on his wrist.

"Where's the escalator?" Sean searched the landing.

"I don't see a way to get down," Melvin called as he ran ahead.

Wyatt eyed thick stainless steel poles that were planted every thirty feet. "There's no way down." He reached out to touch the smooth metal. "Except for these."

"No way!" Sean lifted himself onto the railing. "I love this place. Incoming!" he shouted, wrapping his arms around the pole and sliding to the bottom.

Wyatt cursed and then hefted himself over the rail, his palms heating under the friction as he slid down the tall pole. He heard Melvin screeching from the next pole.

Melvin had a messy landing. He turned to Nolan and demanded, "Which way is it?"

Nolan laughed. "That way, you freak." He pointed down a winding path.

Wyatt landed at the base. Sean waited until Wyatt's feet touched the concrete before he raced off, following the painted signs indicating the way to the werewolf flume ride. Wyatt stood close to the metal pole, the crowd closing in on him. The line had grown even longer, eager people talking excitedly about the attractions.

Nolan impatiently pulled his arm. "Come on. Jade's waiting for us."

They dodged strolling people, running on the uneven cobbles. Melvin disappeared around a bend, and the other three boys followed. Wyatt walked alongside Nolan, who kept the pace brisk. People in Halloween-like costumes roamed the streets, laughing like it was Fat Tuesday in New Orleans. The only things missing were food and drinks.

It was a maze of rutted paths, structures squeezed together from different centuries as if they were plopped down by giant hands. Wyatt noticed the buildings were not abandoned. Sagging wrought iron balconies sported women dressed like a collection of vampires and zombies in different outfits spanning the centuries, from ancient Rome to Tudor times; even twentieth-century flappers were included in the display. It was a strange assortment that jarred the nerves.

Wyatt looked at the merchandise crammed in the windows, hawkers standing outside, their zombie makeup running from the heat of the bright lights overhead.

It was a kaleidoscope of sounds and colors, as if they rode a merry-go-round at breakneck speed. Guards stood every few feet, their emotionless faces revealing nothing. While they did seem robotic, Wyatt had a sense of peace knowing they were there.

Sean ran toward a large glass case that displayed a four-foot-long handle with a polished silver axe at the top.

Melvin skidded to a stop to admire it. "Look at that!" He was so excited he couldn't catch his breath.

"Calm down before you hyperventilate." Wyatt could see they had them installed at the end of every building.

Melvin observed with awe. "He's thought of everything. A silver axe can take out a vampire, zombie, or werewolf."

"Or a human," Wyatt added.

"Why would you even say that?" Nolan snapped.

"Take a picture of me." Melvin mugged a pose by the axe.

"Are you twelve?" Wyatt asked, thinking of Jade waiting at the end of the line. Melvin could be such a baby.

Melvin shook his head, "I'm outta here." He took off in a jog down Werewolf Way.

Wyatt turned his attention to the passing scenery as they continued their trek.

The buildings thinned, turning into a wide lane with dense brush intruding. City sounds receded, drowned out by bird-calls and the piped-in sound of banjos playing. Wyatt saw nothing beyond the line of eager people waiting like a giant anaconda stretching along the winding road.

Soon the concrete was replaced by a dirt path. To the right, he saw a giant glass dome with multifaceted windows.

They slowed their progress, stopping when they noticed a muted figure of a man skitter across the glass.

"Did you see that?" Sean gasped.

"What?" Wyatt asked.

"Something was in there," Sean said, pointing to the dome.

"It's the werewolves; they're isolated behind the glass." Nolan pulled a map from his back pocket. "See that big tube?" He pointed to a thick pipe that wrapped around the side of the dome. "It's a feeding chute. There's a silo back there filled with blood and guts. It goes directly into the zombie town."

"Wow." Sean craned his neck to look at the long pipe.

They all traced the destination of the pipe to find it penetrating an enormous stone wall at the north end of the park. They could make out the armored mesh the employees wore as they walked around the exhibit.

"Wy!" Sean jumped up, pointing. "The zombies, bro. They're right behind that wall."

Wyatt looked at the fortress longingly and then back to where Jade waited for them. He shook his head. "We have all night. Let's go on the River Run."

"You still have that invitation thing?" Nolan asked.

Wyatt nodded.

"I want to see it."

Wyatt took the folded square, handing it to Nolan.

"I bet you it's real skin," Nolan said with admiration.

Wyatt dropped it into Nolan's eager hands.

"Can't be." He shook his head. "It's probably synthetic." Wyatt looked at the uneven texture.

"Skin!" Sean shouted. "Ew, look, hair."

They all peered closer at the invitation. The parchment's ragged border ended in a delicate fray. Wyatt touched it, feeling the coarse bristle of hair. "You keep it." He shoved it to Nolan. "It's probably a pig skin."

"Well, I love me some pig skins." Nolan laughed. "Thanks, man. I owe you one." Nolan bunched it up to put it in his pocket.

"Where's Jade?" Wyatt asked, changing the subject. He wanted to find a place to wash his hands. They itched where they'd touched the fur. He felt disoriented. Nothing made sense in the park.

He had been to loads of theme parks and county fairs. This place was set up as though the planners threw down a bunch of swerved lines and named them as streets. *And tickets to those parks were made from paper, plain old paper.* Wyatt glanced back at the central area of the park, feeling uneasy he was being led somewhere he shouldn't be going.

"Creepy, right?"

Wyatt jumped when Nolan came too close behind him. He moved away. He watched his brother run down the lane, screaming, "Come on, Wy!"

Nolan laughed. "Yeah, come on, Wy."

He studied Nolan, wondering why he was being so nice.

"Jade wasn't happy about being left behind. She's a real scaredy-cat."

It was full-on night now—the moon hung low in the sky, its round face mocking them. The street lamps were flickering eerily, just enough to make Wyatt's skin crawl. The bright light cast an odd glow on people's features so that their eyes disappeared into the shadows of their faces. He thought about Jade waiting in that line and picked up his pace.

Wyatt let Nolan propel him through the crowd, knowing Jade would be at the destination.

Jade stood in the middle of a long maze held in place by metal stanchions. Nolan screamed her name while he waved his arm. She squeezed past the tightly packed people to run to them.

"How do you like it?" she asked, her face scrunched, indicating she wasn't thrilled.

Wyatt pursed his lips, and something passed between him and Jade. He felt her small hand touch his fingers and squeeze them gently. Wyatt looked nervously to see if Nolan noticed, but the jock was preoccupied searching for the entrance to the ride.

Nolan interrupted him. "Look, you can say Jade is Melvin's guest, and I'll go as yours. Otherwise, we're going to have to wait a couple of hours to get on this." He looked around. "Where is that idiot?"

"I'm not going down there, it's dark. You go be Melvin's guest," Jade said.

Wyatt scanned the crowd. "I don't see him. Sean, let him walk next to you."

Wyatt took Jade by the arm and started walking briskly toward the entrance of the ride.

Nolan caught up quickly, matching their strides, so they marched shoulder to shoulder until the path abruptly stopped at the edge of a cove with a waist-high metal gate preventing them from moving further.

Wyatt's jaw dropped when he saw the entire waterway spread out before him. Low hanging branches grazed the iridescent water. Strategically placed spotlights lit up an array of exotically colored flowers that filled the area with perfume.

Jade sucked in her breath, "It's beautiful."

A bird cawed loudly, but for the life of him, Wyatt couldn't find the source of the sound.

"Dudes!"

They heard Melvin's voice from across the water. He was waving wildly from a small mound of dirt on the other end of a rickety suspended bridge. "You have to cross the bridge! It's crazy!!" he screamed.

They stared with dawning horror at a decrepit bridge that swung precariously over the lagoon. Wyatt looked down and saw something dark splash under the surface of the cloudy water.

Melvin yelled, "C'mon, hurry! What, are you afraid there's a creature like from the Black Lagoon?" He laughed at his joke.

"Maybe it's the Loch Ness Monster," Sean said in a rush.

Jade shivered uncontrollably. "That looks dangerous."

Wyatt gulped and wondered why they couldn't get on the boat right there. After all, he did have a Presidential Pass.

"Show me your VIP bracelets," a nasal-voiced attendant demanded. A short, pudgy woman came out of nowhere, startling them. Wyatt raised his arm, showing her the black rubber band. She punched in a code on a keypad, and they heard the pneumatic hiss of a gate being lifted.

To get to the ride, they realized they had to form a single line to cross the decaying bridge that led to the actual entrance of the ride.

"Me first!" screamed Sean, pushing Wyatt out of the way to run across the flimsy looking bridge. It swayed with each step as if the ropes were made of elastic.

Just looking at the narrow slats held together with fragile hemp over the murky water made Wyatt nervous.

"I'm not going on that thing," Jade said, her arms folded across her chest.

"Oh, yes you are," Nolan said, taking her hand and striding across the rickety bridge.

Wyatt watched them cross, his eyes open wide. The attendant said, "I have to close this gate. You better go."

Taking a deep breath, he placed one foot on the slats of the wood that separated him from the water. Fingers gripping the hemp tightly, he moved across.

Instead of lifting his feet, he slid slowly, inching his way to the other side. His gullet met the back of his throat in fear. If the bridge was just the beginning of the ride, he wondered how the werewolves were going to top this.

They saw Melvin eagerly waiting underneath a large

grass-topped hut that was made with green bamboo. A uniformed attendant stood next to him.

Seven passenger boats pulled up on the lee side of their little island, loading the awaiting guests. The flat-bottom crafts were painted bright green with yellow canopies fringed along the top.

"That looks charming," Jade said.

"Looks are deceiving." Melvin turned to face them. He was chewing something.

"What are you eating?" Wyatt hissed.

"Kickers Kandy Bar." Melvin's teeth were covered with melting marshmallow, and his breath smelled of chocolate.

"You can't eat here."

"Stop being an old lady. They feed the werewolves until they're in a stupor. They probably drug them too."

"You don't know that," Wyatt responded

"Of course he does. He'd be stupid not to. Besides, they eat meat. They don't care about chocolate," Nolan told him, as if he knew everything there was to know.

The attendant turned to look suspiciously at the group, who clammed up. "Just get in the boat," Melvin whispered.

The boat dipped into the swampy water as they entered. The attendant helped Jade to the last row of seats on the bobbing craft, directing Wyatt to follow her. Nolan cursed but entered the middle row with Sean. Jade paused, looking back at Wyatt, and then moved only halfway to the end, so that she was squeezed up against him.

Melvin was at the bow. Nolan twisted to look at Wyatt and Jade, his face tight, his eyes narrowed to slits. Wyatt realized he was being watched by the quarterback, and he gulped convulsively. It lasted for a long minute, and, when Nolan finally turned around, Wyatt wondered who scared him more, the monsters in the park or Jade's boyfriend.

The quarterback swung his arm over the seat, letting his hand rest possessively on Jade's knee. Jade's face grew red, and she moved her legs restlessly, but Nolan's hand stayed. The gears hitched and then groaned. The boat pulled away from the dock.

A guide jumped onto the stern, standing slightly above them on a block. He held a mic in his hand and began the ride with a bored attitude. The guide fixed a bush hat on his head, and his khaki uniform had both a werewolf and the Monsterland logo on the pocketed chest. He advised them to belt themselves in. To Jade's obvious relief, the tight fit of the constraints forced Nolan to reluctantly remove his hand.

"Doctor Vincent Konrad has long had a fascination with monsters," the guide began. "Funding the Everglades expedition with his own money, he expected to search for and find Bigfoot, or, as it is known in Native American folklore, Sasquatch."

The boat glided over the water, its bow making arrow-shaped ripples on the still surface of the artificial lake. Shimmering dragonflies hovered over the water, frogs croaked, and the air became thicker. It grew darker, the dense brush growing over the water, the sound hushed.

The howls began, softly at first, and then building in intensity and frequency as the strip of water narrowed. Wyatt had read somewhere that the water ride was behind glass walls to keep the guests safe from the werewolves. He fidgeted restlessly. They were completely out in the open.

The boat rode low in the water. Sean leaned over, splashing the palm of his hand on its flat surface.

"Keep your hands in the boat!" the attendant shouted.

Sean gawped as an alligator swerved close, its long snout snapping open as the boy snatched his hand from the water. He looked up at the guide.

"Indeed, the wildlife is real and not animatronics, as initially reported."

"They're not robots?" Wyatt demanded.

"Dr. Konrad decided that if the monsters were real, so should all elements of the park."

Wyatt felt Jade move close so that their thighs touched. Taking a deep breath, he placed his shoulder in front of hers, as if he were protecting her.

"As I was saying, Dr. Konrad and his staff stumbled upon an unexpected colony, that special May first day. They were in one of the waterways, much like this, when, all of a sudden, they made contact."

The boat lurched sideways, the impact sending them spinning in a half circle. Jade screamed, and Wyatt sucked in his breath, grabbing her by the shoulders and pulling her close. He heard Melvin shout with joy.

The announcer laughed nervously. "With an impact very similar to that, Vincent Konrad made the discovery of a lifetime. He found a pack of werewolves living in—hey!"

The boat was smacked again, this time propelling them almost to the other side of the bank. They craned their necks, peering into the dark water only to see muddled images of something swimming close to the boat's side. The guide reached into his back pocket and whispered urgently into a two way radio attached to the lapel of his shirt.

Melvin released his restraint and stood, pointing to an outcrop of rocks. Wyatt heard Jade gasp. His mouth went dry.

Lining the boulders were five beasts, so large they blocked the light from above. Their long yellow teeth gleamed. Saliva dripped from their mouths like they were rabid. They panted deeply.

Melvin stood at the prow, howling, his eyes closed in ecstasy. Sean pressed himself back into his seat so that his head almost touched his brother. Nolan crouched low.

Wyatt stared at the wolves. The beasts' eyes were bright with intelligence and something else. One walked out so that it was almost above them, his long body quivering with rage. His huge head lifted upward, his mouth opened, letting loose a chilling call. The wolf turned, his eyes narrowing with menace.

The boat stalled and then drifted. The attendant pushed his intercom frantically. He flicked the ignition, and the boat roared to life once again.

Melvin reached up, his face filled with wonder.

"Sit down!" the driver ordered. "Now!"

"Mel!" Wyatt called, breaking his trance. "Sit." He turned to the guide. "Is this part of the show?" he asked frantically. "Is it?"

The man ignored him, his face solemn. Wyatt felt a mixture of fear and the niggling doubt that he was being made a fool.

Melvin slid silently into his seat.

They traveled under the ledge, so close they could hear the uneven panting. Drool dripped onto the boat floor not protected by the canopy.

Jade made a noise, moving so close she was practically underneath Wyatt. Slowly, the boat slid through the water.

Wyatt turned around. The animals were gone, but he felt his scalp tighten. He knew they were watching. Peering through the thick leaves, he searched the foliage but could see nothing. Sean looked back at him nervously.

"That was creepy. Right, Melvin? Mel?" Sean cried.

Melvin was gone.

"Melvin!" Wyatt stood on the rocking boat. The attendant cursed and ran toward the bow, his face white.

The canopy over their heads stretched with the weight of something heavy. Jade shrieked and hid her eyes. Nolan scrambled to move to the back of the boat. A hand dropped over the top of the canopy, a Kickers Kandy Bar clutched in the palm.

Melvin's face appeared under the fringe—he looked like he had blond ringlets.

"Melvin!" Sean yelled.

"I want my money back," Melvin called to the attendant. "It's all fake."

He hopped into the boat, water sloshed over the edge, soaking their sneakers.

"I'm reporting you as soon as we get back!" The employee stomped over to Melvin, making the boat rock dangerously.

"It's a hoax. There are no werewolves. Vincent Konrad is a big phony."

"You can't get your money back," Sean said, pulling the candy from Melvin's hand. "You didn't pay to get in."

"Just sit down," the worker told him.

"Or what?"

"It's the rules." The guide peered behind them, realizing they were creating a traffic jam of boats. "Look, it's going to get better." He scanned the faces in the vessel. "I'll let this incident go. It's opening night, but you must obey the rules. Fasten your belts, please."

Melvin made a rude sound.

"You won't be sorry. I promise."

Melvin hopped over the seats, Nolan slid back into his place, and Jade took Wyatt's hand, lacing her fingers with his.

The ride attendant grabbed the wheel, pressed the throttle, and the boat chugged forward. "It's all real; you'll see."

Wyatt looked back as they passed the large outcrop of rocks, seeing the jerky movements of the wolves, and pointed to them. "They're harmless, Jade. It's not real." He leaned close, whispering in her ear. "It's probably all fake." He felt foolish for being so nervous when he crossed over the bridge earlier.

"You better hold on!" the attendant warned.

The boat suddenly dived down a vertical drop that had to be at least fifteen feet. The echoes of their loud screams sounded canned, as though they were in a cavern.

They landed with a jarring thud that doused them with cold water. Wyatt lost his grip on Jade's hand as they both clung to the rails. The boat rocked, dipping so deep that water splattered over the sides.

Wyatt's eyes adjusted to the dark, misty air. He looked at his brother, who sat with his mouth open, his breath coming in pants. Wyatt was as white as a marble statue, his eyes bulging from his head. He could barely make out Melvin in the front of the boat. Nolan was frozen to his seat, his eyes glued straight ahead. It was pitch black, and Wyatt decided to make the most of the darkness.

He slid his hand over, taking Jade's cold fingers within his own. He heard her expel a deep sigh. He looked sideways and saw a ghost of a smile on her lips. He had the urge to steal a kiss, but it was too risky with Nolan a few feet away. Wyatt squeezed her fingers instead. He felt the softness of her hip next to his.

It was twilight on the bayou, the sound of croaking frogs filling the atmosphere. A motor whined, and the striped canopy rolled back like a convertible on a car, giving them a clear view of the sky.

Jade's head was pressed against his chest. He held her close, their beating hearts pounding in unison. Up ahead, they heard the steady sound of screams mixed with wild howls.

Banjo music filled the cavern. The air was oppressive. Low-hanging Spanish moss dipped into the water. Fireflies lit up the gathering darkness.

"Look up, the sun is setting." The attendant gestured to the manufactured sky.

The lake was covered by the dome, creating a weird echoing sound. The water amplified the splashing of the boats.

The guide gestured to a concave glass barrier above them, separating guests from the werewolves. "That glass is impenetrable. Four elephants can stand on it. It won't even crack."

They heard other attendants repeating the information to their passengers.

"A werewolf can eat four elephants for breakfast," Melvin challenged the guide. Several chuckles emanated from nearby boats.

An artificial sky turned from lilac to purple. The teens watched a thin strip of fiery sunset line the horizon, painting the choppy waters crimson. The sun dipped low and then winked out. The thick glass was transparent. Dark, hulking shadows flitted past them. They discerned the silhouettes of men and heard primitive cries of "No!" mixed with howls that seemed to come from the bowels of hell.

Melvin was out of his seat, causing the boat to rock again. "Werewolves have a superior sense of smell."

Jade looked around nervously. "Do you think they can smell us through the glass?" she whispered. Wyatt placed his arm around her narrow shoulders. She fit against him as if they were made for each other.

He caught Nolan turning around, the whites of his eyes gleaming in the gathering darkness. The boat shuddered violently, and Nolan grabbed the bar in front of him.

This time the attendant's eyes darted around the space above him, his stance alert.

"Come on, already!" Melvin called out. "Show yourself!"

Jade peeked from her haven in Wyatt's arms. Wyatt noticed that Nolan and his brother sat closer together.

Melvin pointed, crowing with excitement.

Pressed against the glass, a man stood, his face a mask of agony, his hands gripping his head.

Wyatt sat transfixed, their eyes meeting, and, this time, he knew the contact was real. He shivered.

The man behind the glass blinked, his eyes turning golden. The LED moon appeared overhead, full, its pocked face mocking the man.

He climbed on the struts holding the dome, lifting his face toward the beacon in the sky, letting loose an earsplitting howl. The veins stood out in his neck; his hand fisted and pounded the glass barrier above them. He wore a thick metal collar, a green pinpoint of a light pulsed under his jaw.

The boat stopped moving. Wyatt noticed four other boats were bobbing around them. Another man jumped onto the rafters, wailing an answering howl, then another. Soon the glass was filled with creatures, their eyes narrowing, their backs elongating. Wyatt and his friends craned their necks to observe as silent witnesses as the miserable creatures' bodies developed four legs, their noses changed into snouts, and their teeth became long yellow fangs. The green lights on their collars multiplied until it looked like the glass was dotted with alien eyes.

He heard Melvin say, "Whoa!"

His breath had stopped in his chest. Jade's brilliant blue eyes peeked out from behind her hands. She sighed, "This is so wrong. In so many ways, it's ... it's wrong."

Melvin stood tall, his chest puffed outward, letting loose a loud howl that silenced the wolves. The water lapped, and only their harsh breathing filled the cavern. Melvin called out again, and a cacophony of cries answered him. His face was ecstatic, and he pumped his fist in the air.

"Stop, Mel." Sean tugged his hand. "You're too weird, dude. Really."

Melvin shook him off, pulled out his cell phone and started filming.

Nolan followed suit and then Sean. Wyatt looked around, noticing everyone had their cell phones in their hands. The lights bobbed in the water as if the room was lit by hundreds of candles. The wolves wailed.

Wyatt picked up his phone and then shoved it back in his pocket. He thought about recording the experience for a second, then paused, his face warming. Jade was right about this place. He felt ashamed for even wanting to preserve a moment on film of another living thing's pain, even if it was a monster.

Wyatt heard the sound of multiple boat engines roaring to life. The attendant yelled, "Hold on!"

They gripped the rails on the seats as the front of the boat lifted half off the water and started racing down a tributary. The water narrowed to a rushing river, the glass coming to surround them like a tube, a handspan above their heads.

Claws scratched the glass, nails clicking as long gray shadows ran next to the boats. Jade screamed, her face inches from the window, a wolf the size of a small car racing in tandem with them. His yellowed eyes watched intently, the golden glow emitting no warmth. The green lights on their collars bobbed along as they chased the boats.

Inhuman wails mixed with menacing growls filled the chamber. Melvin stood, holding onto the metal pole, his face rapt with wonder. Nolan was frozen, his fingers holding the sides of the boat in a death grip. Sean had slid down, his face bleached.

The boat picked up speed, but the creatures kept up the pace; their seven-foot-long bodies and long legs stretched to obscene proportions. Wyatt could hear their impatient snarling. He could swear he felt the heat of their breaths on his cheeks.

Ahead, a pinpoint of light teased them. The boat's speed increased, the wind rushed past them, the wolves howled like mad. One huge wolf dogged their boat, its eyes glued to Melvin. The ride felt endless, like they were going to be stuck for eternity. Wyatt felt trapped.

They were traveling so fast in a downward direction the teens were half lifted out of their seats. Wyatt gripped the handles, his knuckles white. Jade's keening wail filled his ears. A light flashed, blinding them all for an instant.

The boat landed with a large splash in a vast lagoon. The teens twisted in their seats to see the animals slowing, turning to chase after another craft.

Wyatt exchanged a look with his brother and burst out

into nervous laughter. Soon, all the teens were laughing hysterically. Even the attendant joined in, "Don't forget to purchase your photo at the booth on the way out," he added.

"Photo?" Melvin asked.

"Yeah, of your faces as we went down the second waterfall —$59.99 plus tax. Thank you for experiencing Vincent Konrad's Werewolf River Run."

Stark LED floodlights lit up the lagoon. The sounds of the park visitors could be heard again.

Melvin leaped off the boat onto the dock, his face beaming. "That was ah-mazing!" he crowed. "Wanna buy the photos?"

"Not for $59.99." Nolan stepped off, putting his hand in front of Wyatt, rudely pulling Jade from the vessel. "I wasn't that impressed," he said with cocky self-assurance. Wyatt stiffened and then felt himself deflate. Jade was not his girl. She was with Nolan. He backed away.

Melvin wandered off, pulling out his wallet. "Well, I want them," he mumbled to no one.

"Are you kidding me? That was intense. You were a wreck," Sean said to Nolan.

Jade looked longingly at Wyatt as Nolan brushed past them. "Let's try to find Theo and Keisha," Nolan said, dismissing them.

"And Howard Drucker," Wyatt added.

"Did they answer anybody's texts?" Jade asked.

Chapter 15

"Look, Howard Drucker." Keisha pulled Howard into the commissary, separating them from Theo. "I'm tired of waiting for you to notice me."

They both jumped as the doors slowly descended, alarms warning the crowd away from the hermetically sealed portal. They turned in silent awe as the thick metal slid into place, followed by a sucking noise.

Howard spoke as if he hadn't heard her, his voice filled with curiosity. "It's a vacuum."

Keisha wandered to the sealed door, momentarily diverted. Her love for science overtook her hormones and attraction to Howard. "Nothing gets in or out." She ran her hands along the smooth surface of the vulcanized seal. "Not any odors."

She turned, looking at her shorter companion. She considered the gentle slope of Howard's shoulders, the lightly freckled complexion, his total lack of animal attraction, and, yet—she shrugged—she was attracted. Not mildly, not slightly—there was no denying it—she was in a total overload of obsession for this peculiar boy.

While she could explain magnetic shifts in the polar ice caps, she couldn't understand her primal desire for Howard Drucker, but he filled her every waking moment with his keen intellect and sensitive understanding of anything from climate change to the study of chiaroscuro in Renaissance art.

A guard smiled. "Dr. Konrad created this seal especially for the comfort of the inhabitants. Not only the odors but sound as well."

Howard nodded. "The mere sound of food would trigger all sorts of responses."

Keisha agreed, "Like Pavlov's dogs."

"Huh?" The guard cocked his head.

"A Russian scientist proved that if you ring a bell every time you feed a dog, it conditions the animal to associate the sound with feeding time," Keisha informed him.

The guard shook his head. "I don't think those monsters need no bell."

"No, you see," Howard explained, "it was an experiment." He paused to look at the guard's glazed eyes. "Oh, forget it."

Keisha pulled him toward the line that served cafeteria-style food. The restaurant was called Blud & Gutz.

Howard stopped short. "You sure you want to eat here?"

"It's fine, it's just a gimmick."

The servers were dressed in medieval costumes with plague makeup. There were stations filled with massive amounts of hot food from pizza to roast turkey.

"What about one of the other places?" Howard pointed to *La Petit Beast*, a fine dining establishment that was cordoned off in readiness for distinguished guests.

Keisha rolled her eyes and said, "We can't afford it. I bet The Skullery is too expensive for us too."

Howard looked at the casual coffee shop and nodded, "You're probably right."

The noise level in the hall sputtered and then grew silent. A huge group of men in suits were escorted by uniformed officers toward *La Petit Beast*. Vincent Konrad walked with President McAdams, followed by ambassadors, military types, and others in the retinue.

"Wow, President McAdams," Howard said with reverence.

"I wouldn't mind eating with him," Keisha cooed. "That would make for some interesting conversation."

Howard pulled back. "Don't you want to wait for the others?"

"Do you have to do everything with Wyatt and Melvin, Howard Drucker?" She moved closer to him. "Don't you ever want to do anything on your own?"

Howard shifted nervously from foot to foot. "We're hardly alone." He gestured to the crowds rushing around them. He felt strangely naked here with Keisha. What could she possibly see in him? He winced. Words clogged his throat; he didn't know what to say. What if he said something dumb—she would hate him.

Keisha was amazing, from the top of her wild hair to the tips of her toes. She was so smart; she understood Shakespeare like no other student in the class.

Howard gulped, sweat dotting his forehead. Something stupid darted through his usually trustworthy brain. He searched that betraying organ for a clue on how to proceed, and, while it knew every mountain and crater on the moon's surface, it drew a big blank on polite conversation with a beautiful girl.

Howard noticed Keisha's dark eyes survey him, a frown on her face. He was short, so short that he barely reached her shoulder. How could he even think she would be interested in a guy like him?

Howard had a wry wit, but the pithy remarks dried on his parched tongue. The room narrowed to the two of them. His eyes drooped, and he saw Keisha through a strange, spangled veil. He saw her eyes spark and then her lips widened as she moved closer to him. She was so close their breaths intermingled, and Howard swore his glasses were fogging up.

He couldn't stop the next remark in the same way he couldn't fight the tide or the pull of a full moon. "Don't you want to see the vampires?" he whispered.

"Are you kidding me?" Keisha hissed with disappointment, then added, "You and your useless vampires, Howard Drucker."

The meal bell rang, and an announcer came on the PA, warning people to throw out their garbage and reminding them not to take anything into the park. The lights flickered, and the startled crowd gasped in dismay.

"Looks like their electrical system isn't functioning in coordination with the rest of the facilities."

Keisha sighed. "I can name another system that's not working in tandem either."

"Really?" Howard looked around eagerly. "What else have you noticed?"

Keisha groaned, stalking to the entrance that was now sliding open.

"Keisha!" Howard called after her. "I noticed something funny at the escalators as well."

Chapter 16

Sean was glued to a window on the main street of the faux village.

"Tattoos! Wanna get one?" he asked with excitement. Inside the store, patrons dressed like vampires worked at different stations and on various body parts.

"Yeah, sure, and watch Mom's head spin like she's possessed?"

"She'll never know. Besides, she has one," Sean persisted.

They both smiled at the thought of their mother's faded tribal tattoo on the small of her back.

"Yeah, but she subscribes to the rules of do as I say, not as I do. Anyway, Carter's X-ray vision will see it."

Sean nodded. "Yeah, Carter. He may find everything, but he's not our dad. He has no say in what we do, nothing! If I want a tattoo, I'll get one, and he can't do anything about it." He changed the subject. "Okay, what else do they have here?"

He moved to enter the doorway of the next shop. Wyatt followed him into the dark interior. Racks filled with shirts, sweatpants, and hats with the Monsterland logo closed in on them. It was packed so carefully together; they had to turn sideways to meander around the store.

Sean held up shirts, laughing. *I Survived Monsterland*, with werewolf claw marks that glowed in the dark. A baby's onesie had a picture of an infant zombie on it with the words *Feed Me Now*. Wyatt held up a red thermos with an animated cartoon vampire that had a bloody liquid encased by plastic.

Wyatt moved things out of the way to look at the merchandise, faintly annoyed at the commercial bent of the store. *Wasn't this supposed to be a place for observation, not exploitation?*

"See something you like?" The girl had white makeup on her face, with open sores to look like she had the plague. Her fingernails were painted blue, with the telltale white spots of the disease marring the surface. Her hair hung lank, with huge bald spots that were made by latex. Her irises were covered by black contacts, the whites covered with something to make them look bloody.

"No," Wyatt said.

"Don't you want a sweatshirt?" She held up a thick gray sweatshirt that was too short in the midriff. It was shoddily made. She laid it across the top of the rack so Wyatt could appreciate the humor of its joke.

"See ..." She pointed. "It says *Keep Calm and Monster On.*"

"I see what it says," Wyatt responded. "Whose idea was all this?"

She stared at him oddly. "I don't know." She shrugged indifferently. "Who cares? You interested or not?"

Wyatt shook his head. Sean came running over. "Look at this; isn't it cool?" He wore a white T-shirt that sported a cartoon and the saying *The Zombies Got Me* with illustrated entrails printed on the shirt.

"Why'd you buy that?" Wyatt asked as they left the store.

"Are you kidding me? I'll be the first one wearing this."

Wyatt stopped in the street, his eyes stinging. He stared at the bleak town, guests gawking at the windows, the glazed look of shock. People were paused, filming with their cell phones. Signs pulled at him—buy this, purchase that. *Really, what is so special about this place?* He thought for a minute. Each of the main attractions was a tragic example of life gone wrong through sickness or disease.

Wyatt turned to see a monitor across the way. It was a six-foot screen showing images of the Vampire Village. Pale faces filled the TV, their dark, sunken eyes vacant. A hunchback danced around four vamps who played various instruments lethargically.

Scan watched the screen, transfixed. "I heard about them," he said to Wyatt.

They made sound rather than music. It filled Wyatt's head and created a drill behind his eyes. The light hurt, and his chest vibrated with their pulsing melancholy chords that played in monotonous repetition. They were horrible. Looking at their bland faces, without a spark of humanity, was like watching wax figures. *They are no better than zombies,* Wyatt thought wildly.

He turned suddenly, now looking at a screen broadcasting the River Run. Howling figures clamored under the glass dome, their frantic cries filling the street. People stopped and pointed, watching with eager anticipation for the artificial moon to appear and make the men change into beasts.

As expected, the moon rose, pulling the figures into a nightmare. Wyatt spun, looking at the faces enjoying the trans-formation. *Did I look like that?* he thought with disgust. His stomach churned, a seed taking root in his gut, making him close his eyes with horror, not at the beast but himself.

He suddenly realized he hated this place. "It's ... it's ... it's ..."

"It's amazeballs," another voice finished. An arm snaked around his shoulders, much like Vincent and the president. Wyatt shrunk under the weight of it. It was Nolan.

"I've been looking for you everywhere. Hey, nice shirt, Seanie," Nolan shouted. "Anyone hungry?" He thrust a bloody, dismembered hand in Wyatt's face.

Wyatt felt the air leave his body as a buzz sounded in his ears. Nolan held him in a firm grip, shoving the slimy hand toward his lips. "Stop!" He feinted to the left, but Nolan's grasp grew tighter. He could hear Jade's voice imploring Nolan to let go. Nolan's raucous laughter filled his ears, then Nolan cursed, dropping the fake hand to land at their feet.

"Ow, you turd. What'd you do that for?" Nolan rubbed his reddened arm.

Wyatt looked up to see his brother tense, fists raised and eyes narrowed. "My brother told you to stop."

Nolan pushed Sean in the chest, but the younger boy stood firm. Wyatt tried to come between them. "What kind of a wuss are you? You need your little brother to fight your battles?"

Jade had a hand on Nolan's chest, stopping him. She spoke softly to calm him. Her blue eyes were anxious. "I want to leave." She glanced back at Wyatt, her face filled with despair.

Nolan watched their exchange, grabbing her hand possessively. "Not yet. We haven't seen the zombies."

Sean pushed Wyatt's shoulder, rolling his eyes at Jade.

Wyatt shook his head. He heard his name being called. He turned to see Carter moving slowly toward them. Carter seemed troubled. The boys separated, pasting friendly smiles on their faces.

"Problem?" Carter asked, observing the kids.

"No," Nolan picked up the dismembered hand. "I bought Wyatt a gift for getting us onto the rides so quickly." He took Wyatt's hand and slapped the rubber replica into his palm. "Thanks for giving us a hand." He laughed. He turned to grab Jade by the elbow. "You going to Vampire Village?"

Wyatt nodded. "In a minute," he replied, the set of his mouth mulish.

"See ya." Nolan made an abrupt spin, dragging a reluctant Jade, and started walking briskly toward Zombieville.

"Carter!" Sean said to his stepfather, his face filled with happiness. "This place rocks. We just did the River Run. They have a fake full moon—"

Carter looked at Wyatt. "You okay?" He glanced down at the souvenir.

"It was nothing. I can handle it," Wyatt said, embarrassed by the attention. "Stop it, Carter. I'm not five." He stared at the floor. "What are you doing out here? Where's the president?"

"I'm on break." Carter's gray eyes studied the crowd, coming to rest on a trio of guards at an entrance. "What's up with that Nolan kid?"

"He's the most popular guy at school." Wyatt shrugged. "He thinks he's funny."

"Do you want me to—"

"I said I can handle it," he repeated, his mouth set in a grim line.

Carter raised his eyebrows but didn't respond. He continued to watch the guards, his face frowning.

Wyatt moved closer, turning to see where Carter was looking. "What?"

"I don't know. A feeling."

Wyatt looked up at the strong face. "What do you see?" Wyatt's phone vibrated with several messages. He glanced at it and smiled. "Finally. Howard Drucker, Vampire Village in five minutes."

Sean whooped. His attention was diverted by a small parade of characters walking through the park. Some were on stilts, others in a rolling float. It was a pretty anemic show, Wyatt thought contemptuously. They were just people dressed in costumes to look like the monsters. At this point, he didn't know what he expected, but it wasn't this … this charade.

Carter gestured to the guards. "Wyatt. Anything seems odd to you?"

Wyatt studied the crowds. He glimpsed back to Carter and saw his gaze resting on a group of guards.

Wyatt considered the three uniformed men that stood like silent sentinels at their posts. They reminded him of something. "They're like those guys in England that guard the Queen. No emotion."

Carter nodded. "They seem lifeless. Robotic."

"Are they all like that?"

Carter thought about the question. "No, the ones inside were more … normal. It's probably some gimmick for the masses."

Wyatt peered at the blank faces of the three guards. "Doesn't do much to make me feel safe. Vincent is…"

"What?" Carter looked him full in the face. He seemed to want Wyatt to confide in him, to come and ask for advice. Wyatt paused. He couldn't do it.

Wyatt shrugged. "I … I don't know. It could be hype. We saw a video. It might not have even been real," Wyatt said in a rush. "I can't believe that Dr. Konrad could have bad intentions."

Carter laughed. "Yeah, sure." He ruffled Wyatt's hair.

Wyatt pulled his head away, annoyed.

"Look, if it gets crazy in here, just break the glass of one of those emergency cases and use the axe," Carter said, his voice serious.

Wyatt held up the silicone hand that Nolan gave him, and wiggled it. "I'll throw this at the zombies if they attack."

"You want that?" Sean asked.

Wyatt shook his head and then considered his brother. "*You* want it?" he asked, disgusted. Sean nodded eagerly.

Wyatt handed him the fake appendage. Sean smiled, grabbed it, and turned to enter the next attraction.

"Hey, Sean," Wyatt called. "Thanks for watching my back."

Sean grinned, and, for a minute, he looked four years old again. He said, "I bet now you're glad you let me come. Let's go see me some vampires!" He waved, running off to enter the Vampire Village.

"Looks like you're getting along better," Carter murmured.

Wyatt cocked his head. "I can't stay mad at him. He's my brother. Family." He paused, becoming uncomfortable. "Other than the catatonic police force, do you like the place?"

Carter's deep-set eyes squinted in the harsh glare of the lamps. "Not my kind of thing." He considered Wyatt. "What do you think of your idol now?"

Wyatt was silent. He didn't have words. Thoughts roiled in his head, taking shape and then disintegrating. Hazy ideas clashed with firm beliefs until all he felt was confusion coupled with his longing to sit with Jade, feel her soft hand, place his arm around her shoulders. Wyatt closed his eyes in abject misery.

Carter was eyeing him skeptically, and Wyatt was glad he chose to stay silent.

"Wyatt, if it's any consolation, Jade didn't look like she was too happy with Nolan either. Let her know you're interested."

Wyatt made a face but didn't respond. "What's next on your schedule?" he asked, changing the subject.

"I've been selected for the president's detail to accompany him on the rides. He's eating now. We're waiting for him to finish." The radio on his hip gave a static squawk. "Duty calls." Carter pushed away from the stanchion on which he was leaning. He paused for a minute and turned to look at Wyatt. "Watch out for your brother."

"Why?" Wyatt asked.

"Because I said so," Carter said with a chuckle. "That's what a father is supposed to say, right?"

"Yeah, sure," Wyatt said, a look passing between them. Carter seemed expectant, even hopeful, but Wyatt couldn't do it. His mom wanted them to call him *Dad*. He opened his mouth to try it out and then changed his mind. He looked around as if he realized someone was missing. "Did you see Melvin?"

Carter sighed, pointing behind Wyatt's shoulder. Wyatt turned to see Melvin running in his awkward loping strides, disappearing down the road leading to the Werewolf River Run again.

Wyatt shook his head. "I gotta go. See ya, Carter." He jogged toward his friends waiting at the entrance of the Vampire Village.

Chapter 17

Billy had smelled the intruder before he saw him. The moon was fully out now, its bright light seeping in through the tinted glass. He didn't need to see it to know its power, he thought grimly. His pointed ears perked up at the sound of the clumsy limbs thrashing in the grass.

He looked at the camera rotating on its axle. Counting silently in his head; Billy knew he had four minutes left before he had to move. The guard, Billy recently decided to call him Catfish because he smelled like three-day old fish, was due to walk through this portion of the glade. Little John named the other guard Snake.

Billy had slipped away when the president arrived. All the personnel had lined up for handshakes and introductions. Almighty Vincent was there, his hand on the president's shoulder, his wide smile revealing his large teeth.

Billy and his pack used the key card to slip out of their dens after the last feeding. Billy got out first, using his fingers clumsily, and then released the others. The actual full moon outside the lighted dome did its work changing their forms, and now they were waiting. Waiting for the right moment to take back what was stolen from them—their freedom.

He backed into the dense brush, his eyes alert. The air was heavy with their scent. He fought the urge to howl; he didn't want to give his spot away.

He heard Petey and Little John rushing up the other side of the hill to get into position. He thought about the plastic key tucked into a corner. If he reverted to human form, it would come in handy. If only it would work on this blasted collar.

He rubbed it against a tree, but it was on tight. The green light burned a hole into his retina. He rolled in the dirt, hoping the dust would dull the brightness.

He heard talking.

"Where'd they go?" Catfish was asking. "I don't see any of the collars." He checked the dense greenery. "I told them they should have made the lights a different color."

"They're probably taking a crap in the woods," the one they called Snake responded. "How'd they get out of the pens?"

"Nothing's broken. It's like they had a key or something." Catfish shook his head. "Unless you forgot to lock 'em in before you finished."

"It was locked," Snake said. "Have you alerted security?"

Billy watched Catfish glare at Snake in a silent standoff. Peering through the bushes, he knew Catfish was squirming over his missing key. He snickered under his breath.

"Yeah," Catfish replied. "Security will be looking for the beasts on the cameras."

Billy spied his friends, their eyes meeting in silent communication. Little John grinned, his long teeth dripping with saliva in anticipation of the kill.

The beasts simultaneously crouched, their long nails scoring the packed dirt.

Black boots came closer, planting themselves right in front

of Billy. He watched the moving camera rotate in the other direction.

A howl erupted from Billy's throat. He leaped up, sinking his fierce teeth into the soft skin of Catfish's neck, cutting off his vocal cords, so he died quickly and silently. The blood spurted like a fountain, the man's groan dying in his throat with a muffled gasp. His hands scrambled with the weapon at his hip, but his torn throat cut off the air so efficiently that he was dead before he hit the ground.

Billy tore deep into his chest, feasting on the slowly beating heart. His face was damp with blood, and his eyes alight with triumph. He saw that Little John's front paws were deep into Snake's chest, his snout pulling at muscles and tendons with keen relish.

He howled again, telling the others of his victory. Heavy feet intruded into his glen. He spun to face a younger person, his frizzy red hair a fiery nimbus around his face. The boy stood transfixed, his eyes full with something, but Billy knew it wasn't fear.

Billy trotted toward him. He heard an exhalation of breath, and the boy locked his gaze on the wolf in admiration.

The teen held out his hand in supplication. Emerald eyes from a gold pendant winked in the gloom.

Billy heard Little John snarl as he leaped forward, knocking the boy in the chest. He raced over, pushing the other wolf out of the way.

"He's mine," he growled, declaring his territory. He nipped Little John's neck. Little John backed away, subdued.

He turned, his long fangs gleaming in the moonlight, blood from his victim dripping from their sharp tips.

The boy reached out again, his eyes filled with longing. He gripped the fur and then patted it gently. Billy paused; The vibration, the life's blood pounding in the boy's fingertips, danced in time to his own beating heart.

The teen whispered, "I need to belong somewhere. I want

to belong." He held out a grubby hand with something in it. "Want a Kickers?" he asked softly.

Billy opened his mouth and let loose a primal scream. The boy's jaws opened wide, and he joined him, their howls echoing in unison.

Billy crouched, his eyes moving to the camera. He growled in surprise when he saw ripped wires dangling where the mounted lens used to be. The boy held out his other hand, the decapitated camera in his palm, and smiled.

"Looking for this?"

Chapter 18

Carter returned to his detail in the main control rooms to stand behind a group of politicians. Vincent Konrad was back, answering questions as he continued to show them the back lot of the park.

"Impressive," President McAdams said. "The whole place is impressive. Quite a setup you have here. Excellent meal, by the way."

General Anthony shook his head.

"Something wrong, General?" Vincent asked.

The general put his hands behind his back as he walked to the front of the group. "Not my style, this whole thing."

"You don't agree with the idea of placing the monsters in parks to be observed?" asked the Norwegian ambassador.

"Our park is opening tonight as well," the French minister said. "This is unprecedented. Seven theme parks opening simultaneously. The entire world banding together to combat these parasites is nothing short of a miracle."

"Indeed," the Russian ambassador agreed. "This proves the world can cooperate to solve the problems facing our globe."

Vincent nodded. "As you can see, my monsters are in a regulated situation with identical controlled circumstances in all locations. What we've done here is being duplicated in each locale."

"We had the plague victims in a controlled situation. No, sir, this whole thing is a circus," the general replied, proving to be a hard sell.

"Come now, General Anthony," McAdams said. "This was a perfect idea. Dr. Konrad is happy to take on the expense. The world economy was at a standstill with the effects of the plague. It cost our government a fortune to keep the victims separated."

"It's exploitation of people who are ill."

There was grumbling around the crowd. Carter silently agreed with the general. Senator Chiswick turned abruptly. "Would you rather let them all die, perhaps? Dr. Konrad is a national, no, I meant to say a *world* hero. He has tackled a problem that froze both the House and the Senate for over two years. Do you want to go back to that? The entire world was at an impasse. The debate over what to do with the plague victims polarized the government so that no bills were passed for over two years. Vincent Konrad saved this country." Chiswick pointed his finger into the air. "We were bordering on a civil war. Half the population wanted them exterminated!"

The general looked at the screen. It was the Vampire Village. A theater was lit up, with a group of pasty-faced people strutting across the stage. The audience was laughing, enjoying the antics of their performance. Dressed in macabre interpretations of eighteenth-century brothel wear, they rocked the stage, belting out popular songs with exaggerated movements.

"It's humiliating."

"For whom?" Vincent asked, his dark eyes boring holes into the general. "They were invisible in society, drinking animal blood, hiding in the dark, waiting for the unwary teenager to stumble in and be initiated into their group. Now teens are safe. The predators are locked up, under guard. They can be a cautionary tale to the unwise adolescent."

Carter observed the mesmerized crowd moving in coordination with the singer and his raspy voice. The camera panned the audience. Their rapt eyes held the performer. Hips gyrated, hands clapped, voices shouted back the words. They were worshipping their new rock stars.

Carter watched a tech discreetly tap Vincent on the shoulder. His taut face conveyed a message that caused Vincent's lips to tighten. Vincent excused himself quietly to go to a console in the far left corner.

There was a commotion around the computer, which resulted in a small argument. The doctor seemed to assert himself, silencing the problem. In a flurry of activity, employees rushed out the door, whispered commands following them.

Vincent twisted, smiling in a reassuring and condescending manner, telling the room at large, "Opening night snafus! My capable and experienced team is resolving the issues. You have the added privilege of seeing Monsterland at its best."

President McAdams started to clap; the rest of the guests soon followed so that the room was filled with resounding applause. The doctor beamed benignly.

"I would like to mingle with my guests in the park. Perhaps you would like to attend the River Run ride?" Vincent asked the president.

Carter pushed himself away from the wall. He looked back to the worried face of the tech on the computer where Vincent had been. He shivered involuntarily.

Carter suddenly regretted that he hadn't sent the boys home. He hurried after the president and his detail.

Chapter 19

Vampire Village was a techno paradise, all gleaming chrome and monochromatic buildings in neutral gray. Everything had graffiti, artfully drawn cartoons of pasty-looking subjects with large soulful eyes.

There were no cobbled streets here; recycled tire rubber lined the ground, and the buildings grew out of the black depths to stand like monoliths, their smooth surfaces polished to a dull pewter. The village was created around a circle instead of a town square. There was a screen with a count-down clock for the next show time. Stores lined the curved street, selling garish Goth clothing, peculiar hats, and shoes that would make Frankenstein's monster feel right at home.

The teens met up at the entrance. Wyatt looked from Keisha's unhappy face to Howard Drucker's enthralled one.

Theo popped out from behind a doorway and said, "You ditched me at the commissary!"

Howard Drucker shook his head, and said, "No, we didn't."

"Yes, we did," nodded Keisha with a smirk.

"What'd you guys see?" Wyatt asked.

"I was at the zombie shooting gallery near the entrance of Zombieville." Theo said.

"We did nothing." Keisha shrugged her shoulders. "We didn't see or do anything."

"We saw McAdams eating."

"Awesome," Sean responded. "Did they feed him anything cool, like a body part?"

"Don't be a jerk." Keisha dismissed them to walk ahead. She was miffed. The others followed her long-legged strides.

They wandered like tourists through the wide doorway of *Undead Threads*, a clothing shop filled with dark and brooding clothing that would appeal to the vampire-minded.

Wyatt saw Keisha's eyes light up with mischief when she spied an attractive mannequin on a pedestal, dressed in a ripped T-shirt, and skintight leather pants that were heavily studded with sharp metal tacks. She giggled as she poked the figurine, her jaw dropping when the mannequin poked back.

"They're all real," she exclaimed, her eyes bright. The vampire was shockingly beautiful, taller than Keisha, no easy feat. His pitch-black shoulder-length hair was parted down the middle. His eyes were dark pools of indigo. He had elegant fingers, with razor-sharp nails that captivated the girl. The man had an indecent mouth, mobile with a lazy grin that seemed to be only for her.

"What are you talking about?" Howard asked.

"The mannequins, they're vampires!" Sean pointed. He approached a towering Asian figurine with silky purple hair covering half his face. Sean reached out to tug his long military coat.

"See something you like?" asked the figure, bending down to eye level. He swung his hair in a wide arc revealing a face filled with anger mixed with contempt. His lips opened with a sneer, exposing sharp fangs.

The group reared back, Keisha stepping onto Howard Drucker's feet. He steadied her, but she pulled away, moving closer to the leather-clad vampire, who jumped down from the pedestal.

"Who's your little boyfriend?" He walked to a female mannequin, took her hand and helped her off her stand. They circled the group. "We won't hurt you." He threw his head back as he laughed. "We've been capped, see?"

He opened his mouth to show a clear brace covering his fangs, preventing them from doing any harm. "If you don't believe me, ask him." He pointed to the door where Vincent Konrad entered with a large group of people.

"Ah." Vincent snapped his fingers at his assistant, who followed dutifully at his side. "The boy who fed me at that hamburger joint, Billy Baldwin."

"It's Wyatt," he corrected him.

"And look who is playing with him, Diana, the huntress."

Keisha separated herself from the group and approached the older man. "I told you my name is Keisha, not Diana."

"Isn't she pretty, Raoul?" he asked the black haired vampire.

Raoul walked toward the group. "She's a sweet, young thing."

Howard Drucker watched him warily, uncomfortable with the way the vampire was staring at Keisha. He wasn't too thrilled about the way she stared back.

A female came up behind Howard, wrapping her arms around him. He jumped when she touched him, but her strong hands caressed his shoulders possessively.

Vincent separated them. "You're scaring the children, Angie."

Angie narrowed her heavily kohled eyes. "Isn't that what we are supposed to do?" Her dress fluttered around her, the tattered material of her skirt revealing torn fishnet thigh-highs.

"You're supposed to entertain the guests. Angie and Ian,

please escort the Norwegian ambassador and show him where we have blood drawn."

Angie linked her arm with the diplomat, and the pair of vampires ushered him from the shop.

"Blood drawn?" Wyatt asked.

"Naughty boy. If you had stayed with us, you would have learned all about how we maintain the park. Vampires love blood."

"Everybody knows that." Howard Drucker came closer.

"Yes. It's common knowledge. However, the misconception is that they need human blood. Simply not true. Being able to feed on any type of blood is how they've been able to last as long as they have. We use animal blood. Then we feed the raw meat to the zombies."

"No waste." Howard shook his head.

"Correct, young man. We keep them sated. They don't crave human blood. Raoul, care to explain?"

Raoul approached Keisha. She was almost as tall as him, her dark skin a foil for his white complexion. He reached for her hand, raising it to his lips, twisting it gently so he kissed the inside of her wrist. His eyes never left her face.

Howard's jaw dropped as Keisha shivered, her cheeks flushed.

Raoul stood next to her, his pale fingers caressing her bare arm, raising goose bumps. "We only crave human blood when we mate." He smirked at their shocked faces. "When we are attracted to someone, we want to make them one of us." His finger lightly touched the side of her neck. "That's why our numbers are dwindling. We have not been allowed to mate." Keisha closed her eyes, swaying slightly, baring her elegant neck.

"Imagine that, a life without sex." Vincent commented.

"They can mate with each other," Howard said, his voice cracking.

He moved closer to Keisha, but Raoul looked at him with a sneer. Howard's chest caved inward.

"Boring, boring, boring," Raoul replied. "Could *you* eat the same meal over and over again? Even macaroni and cheese would get tiresome."

"Oh, you crafty devil." Vincent laughed, reaching out to pull Keisha away. "You see what he is doing?"

The people in the crowd blinked owlishly. "He's seducing you," he said, as if sharing juicy gossip. "That is how they increase the population."

"Wait!" Sean called out. "Are you saying they don't bite people all the time?"

Raoul and Angie laughed, and Vincent chuckled alongside them.

A man wearing a military uniform stepped forward. "That's been proven a long time ago. Vampires flew under the radar for years, not being noticed. They only recruit when the flock thins out."

"But it's been designed to diminish now," Wyatt said. "It's illegal for them to bring anyone new into their numbers. The population is dying out."

Raoul turned to stare at them, his face bitter. "Rather unfair, if you ask me. We only initiated those who *begged* for it," he said, his voice a caress on Keisha's skin. "It's when we are at our most seductive … and dangerous," he finished on a purr.

"What?" Howard demanded. Instead of seeing the vampire, all he saw was Keisha's captivated expression as she looked at the monster. *Maybe it wasn't such a bad idea that sex was forbidden for them,* he thought, taking a big gulp. His Adam's apple moved convulsively.

"Little boy." Raoul walked over to him. "We are not indestructible. We are beings, like anybody else, forced to hide because of the misconception. When we thin out, or—" He walked past Keisha, his eyes holding hers "—*recruit*, that's when we become driven." He said with a menacing hiss.

Howard stared back, his body tense, his expression hostile. Wyatt and Sean came up behind him. The room was thick with silence, as if, somehow, sides were drawn.

Vincent checked his watch. "The show is starting momentarily. Move along, you don't want to miss it." He exchanged a look with Raoul, who glanced at Keisha and then nodded to Vincent.

Vincent's assistant rushed the patrons toward a group of performers milling in the center of the circle. A hunchback dressed in dark clothes waltzed around, teasing, juggling, entertaining the crowd. People were amused by his antics.

Vincent glimpsed outside the store's entrance, motioning Raoul over. "Not on opening night."

"It's only fair. She will make an attractive addition, unlike that fool." He pointed to the hunchback who was doing headstands. He was wearing so much face paint; the actor's features were a garish mask. He was barely recognizable as a human. "Vincent, what were you thinking?"

"I was thinking of our future," Vincent answered. "He's a favor, nothing more. If you knew who he was connected to, you wouldn't think about questioning it. Don't draw any more attention to him than you have to."

"We don't like him. There's been talk of … you know." Raoul pointed to his fang.

"That would be a shame." Vincent shook his head.

"You said you would give us creative control," Raoul said, his eyes flashing.

"That is true, but you agreed to my terms. I'll arrange something soon to rid you of the creature." He studied Keisha. "I'll make it sweet for you."

"I do want her."

"That's why I gave her a ticket. Patience, Raoul. Entice her. One day at a time, my boy. I like giving you challenges. It will make your time here ..." Vincent searched for a word. "Fun. Use your charms. She'll be back. It's opening night; you have many other nights to recruit her. Seduce her, and she'll be back." He glanced at Sylvie. "Don't they always come back?"

Raoul smiled, his fangs showing. "Yes. Once they have a taste, they always return."

Outside of the store, the hunchback skipped to Sean, where a crowd gathered. "Good evening." One arm hung as if dislocated from his shoulder. He peered up at the boy, a dopey look on his painted face. Sean backed away. He had a broad smile with long, discolored teeth.

"Are you a vampire?" Sean looked at him carefully.

"Hardly," the hunchback answered witheringly. "I am a performer."

"Is that thing real?" Sean pointed to a misshapen lump on the man's right side. "Are you a zombie then?"

"Why, yeth," he lisped. "I am real, and, no, I am not a zombie." He snorted, enjoying his performance more than his audience. "Hunchback. But we actually prefer to be called *vertically impaired*." The crowd laughed.

"You're not a character actor?" Theo demanded.

"Do I look like a man in a cothtume?" He mugged for the crowd.

He started to walk away when Wyatt called out. "Um, not really. How's the pay?"

The performer thought for a minute and then said, "The perkth are nithe. Dr. Konrad offerth four weekth paid vacathion."

"Very generous," a man said with a nod.

"And the lunch at the commithary ith exquithit."

"What's your name?" Theo asked with a laugh.

"Why, ith Igor, of courth."

"Igor? Really? Couldn't think of something more original?" Theo rolled his eyes.

"Where's the vampire ride?" Sean asked, bored with the artist.

"Thith way," the hunchback pointed to multiple doorways leading to an interior. "The thow ith about to thtart. Enter the theater at your own rithk." He ran ahead, playing a flute, melting into the crowd.

"I thought this was going to be cool. It's not. It doesn't look like it's a ride," Sean complained as they entered an amphitheater.

"It's a show, Sean," Wyatt said.

"How'd you know that?"

Wyatt nodded to a giant LED display. "Next show is in ten minutes."

"This is gonna suck," Theo said. "Who wants to see a show? Why's the Hunchback of Notre Dame here? He doesn't even go with the scenery, or the vampires, for that matter."

The arena was shaped in a huge oval and felt like it could easily hold hundreds of people. Wyatt and his friends were propelled by the crowd to the very front, inches from the massive stage. The stadium was surrounded by rows of thick white marble columns giving it a majestic feel.

Wyatt gazed at the star-dotted sky, feeling overwhelmed by the size of the venue. Sean was talking to him, but he could barely hear him over the clamoring crowd.

Wyatt shrugged, his mind drifted back to Jade, his fingers still tingling where she had touched them. He thought about where she was, and wished he could be here with her, holding her hand.

He wondered how many people they could squeeze in the theater. He searched for the exit and realized he couldn't find it.

The hunchback climbed awkwardly up the stairs.

"Hello, eager fanth!" His voice blasted from speakers the size of Mack trucks hanging over the stage. Wyatt put his palms over his ears to protect his abused eardrums.

The hunchback went on, "Monthterland welcometh you to the Nightmare Arena, where all your dreamth come true." He laughed. "Thponthered by Kickerth Kandy Barth. And now, for our feature prethentation tonight, Monthterland proudly prethenth our rethident band, The Abracadaverth."

The theater went dark. Strobe lights lit the night sky. Loud music blasted them, surrounded them, the beat so loud it reverberated through their bones.

Chords blared. The vampires strutted across the stage, and the sound of heavy metal filled the air.

"I heard these guys were really old, but they're sort of cool," Wyatt said to Howard. The beat made him start to move. He turned to see his group swaying to the music.

It was primal, carefully staged to grip the deepest, most elemental roots of what made people human, latching on and dragging them into the vampire's soul.

Love bites! Blood unites!

It was a simple song, one sentence repeated over and over again, almost like a mantra.

Love bites, blood unites. It started with Raoul. His deep baritone washed over them. His voice was magnetic, holding them entranced, freezing the breath in their throat. It oozed and slithered around them, like melted chocolate mixed with caramel.

Soon, the audience was shouting the lyrics as if they had become one brain. *Love bites, blood unites.* All around them was a sea of cell phones lighting up the arena. It seemed to captivate them. Even if the words made no sense, the steady stream of guitar and the beat of the drums invaded their consciousness.

"I thought you said their music was dated," Wyatt leaned close to say in Howard's ear. "I've never heard anything like this."

"I … this is not what I was expecting. It's good … in a weird sort of way."

"What?"

"It's not what I have on an old CD at home."

"What?"

"IT'S BEEN CHANGED TO APPEAL ... oh forget it."
Howard gave up trying to talk over the loud sounds. It was not
what he thought they would do. He liked the old campy stuff
better, made them more pathetic.

Raoul strutted across the stage, his long, lean legs going on
forever, his head thrown back in ecstasy. Sexual appeal radi-
ated from every pore of his body. His dark hair gleamed under
the hot lights. His pale white skin sucked the light inward, so
all that they noticed were his black, soulless eyes.

The crowd was wild. Raoul stood before Howard's portion
of the stage. He was powerful. Howard felt a chill shiver down his
back. He looked nervously for an exit, feeling the edge of panic
when he couldn't find one. He then glanced back at his friends.

Wyatt, Sean, and Theo were moving their heads, caught
in the music. Keisha held her graceful hands in the air,
waving.

The lead singer leaped off the stage, landing nearby. He
pushed through the crowd, coming to stand before Keisha,
holding his hand out, palm up; the crowd was completely
entranced. Keisha, her dark eyes half closed, moved sideways
through the mob.

Howard observed in a detached manner, his hands fisting
convulsively, as she pushed her way through the crowds,
placing her palm on Raoul's waiting one.

Raoul screamed with triumph, dragging her toward the
steps. The audience was like a squirming mass, people
jumping in place with the steady beat of the music, repeating
Love bites, blood unites. The erratic lighting touched them and
then moved on to illuminate another perspiring head.

Howard gasped with mounting horror as Keisha was led
onto the stage. The vampires surrounded her, their voices raw
with primal screams. She undulated with the music, rotating

her hips. Raoul moved behind her, his grip possessive on her waist. He pulled her close to him. Keisha swayed, almost falling against him. Two female vampires ran to either end of the stage, clapping their hands overhead, creating a frenzy on both sides of the platform.

Fireworks exploded from the pillars surrounding the arena, bathing the entire place in shades of purple, blue, and green.

Howard could barely catch his breath. His lungs felt like they were trapped in a vice. He pushed his glasses up the bridge of his nose. He felt sluggish, the music moving through him. His anxiety of before evaporated like a cloud, replaced by lethargy, leaving him feeling as if he couldn't move even if he wanted to.

He looked at the eager faces surrounding him. How had he become one with this crowd? He cocked his head, trying to detach himself emotionally. Clinically, he tried to figure out what was happening.

Howard spied the hunchback sitting on an amplifier in the corner. His ugly face was painted more sinister by the shifting shadows. The sharp dark eyes caught Howard's, and he opened his mouth into a wide grin resembling a wicked jack-o'-lantern.

The world narrowed to the two of them, and the hunchback laughed hard then, as if he knew something that Howard didn't. Howard felt panic return, his stomach tightening in his gut until the only thing he felt was the beating of his heart in time to the pounding drums.

A roar exploded behind the teens. They twisted to the rear; their jaws dropped when a vampire wearing huge rawhide wings soared over the arena in a graceful arc.

Wyatt pointed to the other side of the theater and yelled, "Look!"

They turned to see five more vampires gliding toward

them, their leathery wings creating enough wind to cool the overheated crowd.

People were screaming and gasping, some were laughing. The flying vampires were skimpily clad females. Howard wondered how they had the strength to pluck members of the audience up and bring them airborne to the stage.

Screams of "Take me!" filled the air from the spellbound audience.

Underneath their feet, the ground shifted, and the entire amphitheater began to vibrate, as the floor circled in one direction and the stage moved in the other.

The boys grabbed each other's arms as they moved slightly off-balance. Howard and Wyatt felt a tug and stared slack-jawed as Theo was snatched from his spot by one of the flying vampires. Theo's sneaker slammed into the person's head in front of him as he was dragged to the revolving stage.

They watched him being gently dropped, along with other members of the audience, on the platform. He jumped up to dance eagerly with an ivory-haired female vampire. He started to bump and grind, getting into the music.

Theo grabbed the girl around her waist, pulling her to him and planting a passionate kiss on her mouth. The crowd went nuts.

Keisha was up there. She only had eyes for the dark-haired vampire. Howard waved frantically, trying to get her attention, but she remained oblivious to him. The vamps circled her, their eyes piercing, their hands possessively touching her, gripping her arms.

Keisha was dancing provocatively. She swayed, her face caught in a dreamy expression. Panic bubbled in Howard's chest, spreading until his skin tingled, his feet moving restlessly, not in time to the music.

An empty feeling welled inside of him, squeezing into a hard knot that caused the pit of his stomach to burst like an exploding shell into his circulatory system. Howard Drucker was sweating like a pig. His heart began to race. He turned, punching Wyatt hard in the shoulder.

"Ow, Howard Drucker. What's that for?" Wyatt's voice was slurred as if he were drunk. Wyatt tried to focus.

"They've got Keisha!" He shouted over the deafening music.

"What?"

"Keisha. They are crazy. He wants Keisha." He pointed to the lead singer, who held Keisha in the crook of his elbow, the mic in his other hand.

Wyatt looked at Howard's face, the words taking root in his distracted mind. He glanced up at the stage to watch Keisha move in rhythm with the beat, her eyes closed, her head resting on the chest of the lead singer, who sang behind her. Keisha appeared strange, as if she were possessed.

One thought entered his mind. *Jade.* He had to find Jade.

Wyatt watched in dawning horror as an Asian vampire separated himself from the band, dropping his guitar and grabbing Theo by the neck, pulling him away from the female angrily. He lifted him high into the air and swung him against a large speaker, making it reverberate.

People cheered, thinking it was part of the show. Wyatt knew it wasn't.

The stage went black for an instant. When the lights came on, Theo was on the floor, drained of color, his neck at an odd angle. The crowd was so caught up in the hypnotic beat of the music; they never noticed his body.

Wyatt heard Howard Drucker scream, "Keisha!" in a long, loud wail.

Howard was using his hands to separate the pulsing crowd. People swayed in unison, becoming a solid wall, preventing him from reaching the stage.

Wyatt shook himself, calling to his friend. Much as he wanted to find Jade, he had to help Howard first. "Howard!

Wait!" He spun to his brother, grabbing both his arms. "Get out of here!"

Sean ignored him, caught up in the loud music. Wyatt pulled his brother's face, slapping him hard.

Sean made a fist and swung for Wyatt, but Wyatt caught it within his hand. "There's no time. I have to help Howard Drucker. Something's going down here." He shook him hard. "Do you understand me?"

"It's just music. It's cool."

Wyatt held his brother's gaze firmly. "It's not. Something's happening." They both looked up in time to see one of the vampire's plunge their face into the exposed neck of a member of the audience.

"You think that's part of the show?" Sean's voice was little more than a squeak.

"No." Wyatt gave him a shove.

The guard staff began lining the upper walls, their faces red and blue in the strobe lights, staring straight ahead with blank expressions. "I'll meet you by the garage. If I'm not there in a half hour, leave. I'll find you. Got it?"

Wyatt searched again for a lit exit sign, and, after locating one with a sigh of relief, he pushed Sean in that direction. Sean nodded and slid through the crowd. He paused to look at Wyatt once more. Wyatt waved him out, his face taut.

He looked up at the stage. Keisha leaned against the lead singer, her face serene, her neck exposed. Raoul held her, imprisoning Keisha in a possessive embrace. Her arms hung listlessly at her sides.

The music grew louder, Raoul's singing vibrating in Wyatt's head. He closed his mind to the message and started humming the *ABC*s frantically to lock out the hypnotizing words. Howard Drucker was almost at the stage. Wyatt saw his friend haul himself up, propelling himself to Keisha.

Wyatt searched for Theo on the stage and couldn't find

him. The strobe lights blinked, throwing the scene into a frantic, writhing mass of movement.

Within seconds, the audience participants onstage were lying flat on their backs, their faces bleached of color and a bright trail of blood leaking from their necks.

Raoul screamed a high note, his fangs popping out to shine like polished steel in the lights. The caps were gone, and they gleamed like knives. Raoul arced and then plunged, moving to cover Keisha's pulsing artery in her exposed neck.

Howard Drucker moaned, launching himself at the duo, smashing into them so that they fell into a tangle of limbs. Howard pummeled the singer, while Keisha sat in stunned silence, watching them.

The two females threw down their guitars and moved to pull Howard off Raoul as Wyatt reached the stage. Wyatt looked up with the shocking realization that none of the vamps were playing, but the music continued, piped in from above him.

The two female vampires flung themselves at Howard, slamming him against the raised platform holding the drum set, and his head connected with a loud crash. Another male vampire ran toward his prone friend, kicking Howard roundly in the stomach.

Keisha pulled herself onto all fours, shaking her head as if she were waking up. She roared as the two women took hold of Howard's shoulders. She stood, still groggy, and then she leaped on unsteady legs toward the two of them.

Keisha grabbed both their heads with each hand, banging them together. The sound of their skulls meeting was muffled by the music, but the dazed vampires slid into an untidy heap on the stage.

Howard was on the floor, Raoul standing over him, his hands roped around the younger man's neck, squeezing hard. Keisha's eyes narrowed, becoming silvery with hate. Moving fast, she head-butted him, but he held on tight to Howard's neck.

Wyatt attempted to lift himself onto the stage when the lights went out, plunging the room into darkness. People started screaming, both on the stage and in the audience. Wyatt heard the pounding of feet, and he gripped the stage as the mob in the pit pushed past him.

Sirens rent the night, and strobe lights lit the stage. The panicked mass of people tried to escape. Wyatt hauled himself up in disbelief, waiting for the flashing lights to illuminate the darkness once again.

The red and blue lights painted the area, splashing colors against the abyss. It lasted a minute or so, the room emptying as if the guests were stampeding cattle. The last sounds echoed in the blackness.

Wyatt pulled out his phone, bathing the surrounding area with light. His eyes searched the entire perimeter, squinting hard into the darkness, but he could not find anyone on the stage. Theo was missing. Keisha, Howard Drucker, and the vampires were gone.

Chapter 20

Carter took the point position, walking with Jessup, the president, the ambassador from Russia, and different military personnel behind them in a sea of black suits.

On the other side of the park, the pulsing sound of loud music drowned out the roar of the crowd.

Jessup turned with a smile and asked, "Hear that?"

Carter smirked and said, "Must be one hell of a concert."

The long winding path to the Werewolf River Run felt as dark as it was dangerous. Carter rolled his eyes, thinking this was a recipe for disaster. Anybody could be hidden in the foliage. *What the hell were they thinking?*

Secret Service had cleared the VIP line, so, by the time they had arrived at the pneumatic gate, they could see the boats pulling up next to some godforsaken spit of land across a sluggish body of water.

"We have to cross that thing?" Carter asked, his eyebrows rising to his hairline.

Jessup shrugged his broad shoulders and responded, "It's gotta be safe. It's all part of the theme park, Carter."

President McAdams approached, a smile plastered on his

benign face. "Let's get this show on the road, gentlemen!" He clapped his hands once.

Agent Barstoe, the president's lead security man, pointed at Carter and then Jessup. "Cross that thing and scope out the island. Call once it's been secured."

Carter looked at the dirt hill and wondered what island this goon was talking about. He glanced up, then back at the agent. "Maybe you should drop him in by helicopter?" he asked innocently. Jessup gave him a stern look of warning, but Carter couldn't stop himself. "Don't you think that's a safe alternative?"

Agent Barstoe scratched his bullet-shaped head. "There's no room for the chopper to put him down there."

"Yes, yes. All the trees," Carter agreed, trying to keep a straight face.

"I'm waiting," McAdams said, with an edge of impatience.

"Team, go, go, go!" Barstoe said, in a fair imitation of a Marine drill sergeant.

Carter responded like the soldier he once was, sprinting across the bridge that hovered over the muddy water. Jessup's bulk made it dip so that it grazed the surface of the pond.

Carter got to the other side of the bridge, searched the small piece of land and yelled back, "All clear!"

The Secret Service men inched forward, the president sandwiched between the agents. The rope bridge stretched as they moved, shuffling their feet across the loose planks.

Carter watched in amused silence until there was a loud splash. The lead agent yelled, "Halt!"

The president was encased in a huddle; six burly agents sheltered him in a human shield. The external agents' arms were extending like an angry porcupine and directed at the swirling water.

Guns fired rapidly, their flashing muzzles illuminating the darkness.

Carter ran to the shoreline in time to see the shell of a large tortoise roll over; its body riddled with bullet holes. "Turtle down!" he yelled, to verify the kill. Carter and Jessup shared a chuckle.

The agents put their guns away and sheepishly escorted the president to the other side of the bridge. Carter wondered if they were as embarrassed as he was.

"What a bunch of jerks," Jessup laughed. "I'm going to leave you here. I'll prepare the ride exit, just in case any rogue turtles are lurking in the bushes."

Barstoe refused to make eye contact with either Carter or Jessup. Carter was directed to take the front seat, Barstoe in the rear. They rode low in the water—between them, the president, and the extra guards, they were one more than capacity.

The ride was mildly entertaining, Carter thought, very much like any other amusement park ride he'd taken the boys on. He smiled inwardly, noticing the fake wolves on the outcropping of rocks. Carter wanted to know if the kids at least enjoyed this attraction, and he wondered what Melvin's reaction was to the animatronic werewolves. He hoped they weren't too disappointed with it.

Then, they hit the fifteen-foot drop into a hellish lagoon.

They landed with a crash, bumping into an overturned boat, the water oily with blood. Carter knew something was wrong. Something was very wrong.

Bodies bobbed in the water. Carter unhooked his restraint, shouting to the attendant. "Is this part of the ride?"

The guide's startled face told him everything—he was crouched low in the boat. The wolves' howling started as the fake moonrise painted the horizon of the artificial lake.

"I asked you if this was part of the show?" he demanded.

Barstoe yelled an order and the Secret Service agents surrounded the president once again; their guns were drawn, their faces alert.

"No ... um ... I don't ..." The River Run guide reached

down to press the button on his radio. "Lights on. Something's wrong. Code 8, code 8!"

A weird silence descended. Carter saw a floating body in the water. His hand closed on the soggy suit. He lifted—it was surprisingly light. He squinted into the darkness at the face. Gentle moonlight bathed the pasty skin, and Carter gasped when he realized he was holding the arm of the Russian ambassador.

Other bodies floated by, all dead, some with their throats torn out. The boat shuddered with his movement. The corpse rolled away, sinking, the arm detaching in his grip, torn from the trunk to be held aloft by Carter. He recoiled, dropping it into the water to land with a loud splash.

"Down, down, down." The Secret Service agent covered the president with his body. Nothing but the lapping water and croaking of frogs filled the cavern.

Carter leaned over the bow, peering into the darkness, when a large shape leaped from the water, punching Carter in the chest. He landed painfully on the floor of the boat, blood spraying from the back of the craft to soak his shirt. He gagged.

Distantly, through a misty haze, he heard screams and ripping sounds. Howls mixed with growls filled his ears, blotting out everything else.

He pulled himself up, only to feel the hot breath of one animal against his cheek, and another had its back paw on his legs. He caught sight of a gold pendant in the furry neck of the beast, emerald glass eyes winking in the gloom. It teased a memory, but his muddled mind instinctively moved into protection mode.

Carter scrambled up, reaching for the gun at his ankle, the boat swaying drunkenly as the beasts lurched off, pieces of humanity in their iron jaws. He tried to get his balance and, when he fired, the boat leaped with the recoil, sending him crashing against the bow. His head connected with the sharp side of a seat and Carter knew nothing else.

Carter regained consciousness to the sound of blaring alarms throughout the theme park. The boat made its exit from the dark tunnel. He rubbed the bump on his forehead, his fingers coming away stained red. He felt his stomach flip and then Jessup was shaking him.

"Come on, man. Get up. We have to get out of here."

Jessup had one leg on the landing, the other in the boat, his foot sliding on the growing puddle of blood. The hump of a dead body lay on the middle seat.

"The president?"

"Dead," Jessup choked, his voice cracking. "I've never seen anything like this." He pointed to what was left of President McAdams in the middle of the boat.

"You okay?" Carter asked. "Did anything happen out here?"

"Everybody went berserk and ran when the boats started coming out with mutilated bodies. Carter, I don't know how to say this, but I don't understand why you're alive."

Carter grunted. "I don't know why it didn't kill me."

He rolled up painfully, clutching his shoulder. It hurt where that thing, that animal, rammed him. He was surprised it didn't knock him completely into the lagoon.

Carter straightened, scanning the frantic crowds running for the exits. Papers littered the floor; trash cans were overturned; people screamed as they ran from the various shops. The piped-in music played serenely, giving Monsterland a surreal quality, as if Armageddon had moved into suburbia.

"Guards?"

Jessup shook his head. "They're gone."

"Have you called for backup?"

"Cells are working sporadically. I've sent images and messages out, but I'm not receiving anything."

Carter rose unsteadily to his feet. Jessup gripped his elbow and helped him out of the boat. "What do we do now?" Carter asked.

"We gotta get to the control room."

Carter pulled out his cell, reading the last few messages from the boys. They were in Vampire Village.

"I have to see if my kids are still in the Vampire Village." He stared at the yawning opening, the dark confines a velvet abyss.

Jessup nodded. "Five minutes. I'll meet you at that pole." He pointed to one of the shining columns holding up the mezzanine.

A large gray shadow leaped from the depths of the ride, coming to stand before the two men. It had an odd hue of auburn mixed in its iron-colored hair. The intelligent eyes considered them and then growled ominously.

Jessup moved into a shooting stance; the wolf grinned, baring long yellowed fangs, its gleaming eyes feverishly darting around the space.

The wolf crouched as if ready to strike. Its snout was covered in blood, its paws wet. It was not as large as some of the other beasts Carter had seen inside, but the huge head lifted to make eye contact with him. Carter felt a strange dart of recognition. *It couldn't be*, he thought.

Jessup's finger pressed the trigger, and Carter instinctively lashed out, kicking his arm, so the shot went wild. Jessup wobbled before he landed on his backside. The wolf leaped over him into the crowd, the gold pendant of a werewolf head with emerald glass eyes mocking them.

The wolf turned, its eyes meeting Carter's before it ran into the interior of the park.

"What the hell, Carter?" Jessup got up, panting, his face shocked.

Carter picked up the gun, handing it to Jessup. "It wouldn't have done you any good. We need special bullets," he said and ran toward the deserted Vampire Village.

"It could have killed us," Jessup shouted.

"But it didn't," Carter yelled as he took off.

"Wyatt! Sean!" His shouts echoed back at him. He searched the empty shops, then raced through the vacant arena, finding nothing.

His eyes caught the vague outline of a body half hidden on the stage. He wasn't quite sure, but as he moved closer, he confirmed it was a teen propped in the corner against a speaker.

He raced up the stairs, his heart in his throat, falling to his knees beside a dead adolescent.

Carter turned the face to find one of Wyatt's friends, Theo, his body cold.

"No," he muttered. He pulled out his cell and began texting to the kids, demanding, "Where are you?"

The message refused to go through. No service.

Carter took one last look around, then ran toward the steel poles to try to get to the control area.

Chapter 21

Wyatt stumbled through the park. It was pandemonium. Vendors poured out of the stores, banging into people who rushed the exits.

He pushed through the crowds, stopping when a pack of werewolves emerged from the River Run ride like a cattle drive. Snarling, they dove into the frenzied crowd, grabbing limbs. He heard the tear of clothing, people shrieking as their arms were ripped from their bodies.

It was like watching lions hunt on the savannah in Africa. His breath rasped in his throat. He pulled out his phone, opening the messages. Sean was in the garage. "Hurry."

Wyatt ducked into an alcove. Leaning against the cool stucco, he stared at the carnage in disbelief. Sweat ran down his heated face. He wanted to get home. He wanted to run to the safety of his room.

Wyatt typed frantically. "Don't wait. Get out of here."

"No keys."

Dammit! I should have given him the keys. Think. What would Carter tell me to do?

"Walk. Use the wash behind the school."

"Carter told me not to walk there."

Wyatt exhaled and typed, "It doesn't matter now. Don't worry! Go!"

"You?"

"I'll catch up."

He texted Jade, Howard, and Keisha: "Where r u?"

A few agonizing seconds later his phone vibrated. "Help." It was Jade. "We are locked in with the zombies. The guards are gone, we can't …"

"Come on, Howard Drucker. Answer." He cursed. Nothing.

Wyatt typed a message to Carter, hit send, but it came back as undelivered. He banged the back of his head against the hard wall, a rattle of glass catching his attention. He felt the wall with his hand, coming in contact with a box. Shining the light of his phone inside, he gazed with relief at the giant axe.

He scanned the perimeter of his area for anything to break it but came up empty. Ripping off his shirt, he wrapped his hand tightly and then took a deep breath and punched the glass. It broke with the resonance of a rocket, and Wyatt grabbed the handle with both hands, yanking hard. It came away from the bottom, but the top remained firmly in place. His heart beating like a kettledrum, he frantically pulled at the handle, his feet lifting off the floor.

He heard the growl before he saw the beast, the hair on his neck rising as the scrabbling of four paws came closer. His breath coming in short gasps, he twisted his wrist, wincing when the sharp angle of the glass sliced his hand. He felt hot blood drench his palm, the wooden handle becoming slippery in his grip.

The beast hit him from behind, knocking him sideways, but the force lifted him high so that the axe unhooked from its mooring. Wyatt felt it slip from his fingers to skitter on the concrete.

Winded, he rose and then ducked, rolling in a ball as the werewolf pounced on him. The sharp claws grazed the tender flesh of his ribcage, but he ignored it, stretching out, his hands feeling for the elusive handle.

Wyatt's head snapped up, and his vision filled with four hundred pounds of fur and bone, airborne, coming straight for him. He didn't think—he didn't have to.

His hand closed on the smooth wood of the axe handle. He swung his arm reflexively, the silver axe head shining in the blackness. He put every ounce of strength into his arm as if he were hitting a grand slam in the Copper Valley ballfield.

In slow motion, he watched it slice into the gray fur, his momentum forcing it through the dense cartilage so that the barking head was silenced before the brain had a chance to tell the mouth muscles to stop moving. It tore from his hand to travel with the corpse of the monster, looking like the lance they used to bring bulls down in bullfighting.

The animal bounced high, the body continuing its onslaught, but Wyatt forced himself to twist left, missing the impact of the headless werewolf. It catapulted into a bench, pulling it up from the ground where it was bolted. The head landed with a loud *splat*.

Wyatt sat stunned, panting, his legs numb. He pushed himself painfully to his feet, limping toward the dead wolf. He yanked the axe from the body, cursed softly, and then headed toward Zombieville.

Chapter 22

"Find them?" Jessup asked as they ran toward the forest of posts supporting the mezzanine. They had entered the park through the commissary, but it was locked tight. They couldn't go back that way.

"No," Carter said, looking around the deserted street.

People were hiding, and the wolves had spread out. They heard screams, but this part of the park seemed empty. Occasionally, a dark shape flitted by.

Jessup and Carter studied the base of the steel poles, feeling their way around them in the darkness.

"There's no way up," Carter shouted.

"I don't see any exit signs." Jessup looked around and then up. He hugged the pole, trying to inch upward. "They're too smooth to climb."

Carter searched the park, his eyes resting on one of two trash cans. He tried to lift it, but it was bolted to the floor. "Come on. Help me."

Together both men pressed all their weight against the mesh can. Carter's veins stood out on his neck from the strain, his face crimson. The can groaned and then tore off its base. Carter rolled it toward the pole. They spied another one and soon heaved the second trash can so that they now had a structure nine feet tall. Carter hauled himself up, wobbling as he stood, but he used his weight to balance.

Quickly, he stripped his shirt, wrapping it tightly around the pole. Using his feet as leverage, he began to inch his way up the smooth metal shaft. He looked down to watch Jessup climb the garbage cans after him.

Carter paused, sweat pouring into his stinging eyes. He heard his phone ping with a message, but his hands were clutched tightly in his shirt. It would have to wait. Loosening his hold, he jerked the material upward to continue his slow climb.

Emergency lighting had now turned on. Carter could hear screams and closed his eyes at the horror of the sounds of this disaster.

He heard Jessup shout. A huge wolf stood on his hind legs, bright eyes glowing with excitement, its growls turning into frantic barking. Carter started to slide down, Jessup's orders stopping him.

"No. Go. We've got to shut this thing down."

The animal was leaping, its fangs snapping as it lurched up. Another circled the base of the trash cans, nudging them so Jessup swayed dangerously. "Get out of here!" he screamed.

Carter let go with one hand, reaching for his gun.

"Forget it. It won't do any good," Jessup called as the wolf finally grabbed his arm. He fought, pistol-whipping the beast, but it barked stridently, calling for help. Its jaws snapped, clamping on Jessup's thigh, pulling him down off his pedestal. Jessup screamed once, the sound cut off as his throat was torn out.

Carter's eyes closed with disbelief, his gorge rising. His legs shook, the muscles screaming with the strain. His shoulders were on fire, his stomach churned, but he continued inching upward. The sounds of skin tearing filled his head.

The landing came into view, and he hooked his foot over the railing, his arms shaking with the effort. Dangling over the edge, his arms weakened for a moment, but adrenalin coursed through him, enabling him to vault over the barrier to land in a sweaty heap on the floor. With trembling hands, he pulled out his phone to look at the text.

"Sean is on the way home. I will be too as soon as I get Jade. Zombieville."

"Zombieville," Carter muttered.

Rolling onto his knees, he stood on legs that barely supported him. He put his wrinkled shirt back on. Glancing over the railing, he saw the wreckage of his friend. His heart sunk.

The wolves formed a circle below, their intelligent eyes watching him. They bayed with triumph. The green glow of the lights on their collars speckled the park, looking like a field filled with fireflies.

Carter turned, and his feet carried him toward the other end of the tunnel. Lights went on overhead, dim now—a generator supplied the power, he reasoned. The weak light lit small pools of white that chilled him more than full darkness. *If a generator was running the place, where were the support staff?*

His feet echoed in the dark tunnel, his breath loud in his ears. Carter paused, banging on the outline of doors along the wall. No response. He felt for a lock, found a keypad, but his tired mind couldn't recall the numbers he had seen Vincent punch. Frustrated, he headed to the mouth of the tunnel.

He ran toward the entrance, hitting his fist on the metal barrier separating him from the outside world. It reverberated in the confined space with a tinny resonance.

Shouting, he placed his fingers along the seam, straining to separate the two halves. It was locked tight. Carter cursed.

He heard scrabbling at the other end of the tunnel. There was a loud thump, as though a body were hitting the railing. He hugged the cool metal of the walls, moving toward the sound.

He saw the shadow of a wolf jumping, its long claws trying to hook themselves on the glass barrier. It continued its attempts. It had to be leaping forty or fifty feet. Carter cursed again. Dual paws caught, the hind legs scratching against the glass. Carter watched the bared teeth gleam in the minimal light as the beast pulled itself up and over the barricade.

Carter's breath whooshed out of him. He turned, running to the nearest outline of a door that he saw in the hallway. The paws scraped against the tiled floor, the loud panting filling his ears.

He felt the sides blindly for a keypad. Closing his eyes, he frantically tried to recall the numbers Vincent typed into the keypad earlier.

"Five-eight." *There were more.* He pressed his sweaty head against the wall. He could do this. He muttered the numbers again. He moved his fingers over the keypad.

Come on, numbers, numbers. What were those numbers? he thought, closing his eyes, trying to recreate the moment with Vincent. All he saw were those dark eyes mocking him. He slapped his head. *Think,* he ordered.

"Five-eight-forty-five-oh- …" *What was the next number?* He tried again, going for the five.

The animal was picking up speed. Another wolf landed with a thud after reaching its goal. Four pairs of claws clicked on the surface of the floor. There was an additional number to the code; he recalled Vincent had covered the keypad.

A menacing growl echoed behind him. Carter hissed with fear, his fingers punching the keypad, going through the sequence, again and again, his fingers slick with sweat, pressing each of the digits until he got to seven.

The wolf launched itself at Carter, the lock made a noise,

and the door popped open. Carter squeezed in, slamming the door behind him, smiling at the satisfying *thwack* and the arm-numbing vibration of the wolf hitting the steel door. Carter slid to the floor, his back against the abused door, laughing with relief.

Chapter 23

The tunnel was dank. Water from the lagoon dripped from the overhead pipes. It was dark. Here and there, pools of blood coagulated around the battered bodies of the staff of Monsterland. The wolves had done their damage, Raoul told them. Now they were waiting for the chance to finalize their escape.

Howard groaned. His neck ached as if it had been wrung —*well, it had*, he thought. He cracked open one eye to survey his surroundings. His glasses were gone, and everything had a fuzzy quality. They were underground, the belly of the park. He looked up at the pipes, knowing from the muted sound that he was under a body of water, like an aquarium.

He peered around the dark space. Keisha was sitting, her eyes closed, her knees against her chest. A trickle of blood sluggishly oozed from a spot on her neck.

Howard stiffened. Booted feet stood next to his face.

"He's up." A girl with matted pink hair crouched to look at him. She pulled his face from the dirty floor. "I like him. Can I have this one?" she asked with a plaintive wail.

Raoul separated himself from the shadows on the wall. "Not yet, Sylvie dearest. Young Howard here will lead us out."

Howard sat up, groaning. "How did you know my name?"

Raoul smiled contemptuously. He nodded to Keisha. "My drone told me. She told me everything, Howard Drucker." He said the name slowly, savoring it, as if by saying both names they were confidantes, close.

Howard pulled his tied hands, bound painfully behind him.

"What did you do to her?" he demanded.

"Relax, lover boy. She'll be coming out of it soon. I only sipped a bit of her nectar. She won't stay in this state for long unless I maintain a steady diet." Raoul's eyes sparked.

Howard pulled at the ties confining him, finally giving up, exhausted. "What is this place?"

"Vincent's idea of a *scary* roller coaster attraction. It remains unfinished but one day he intends to frighten the kiddies with trolls and dragons," Raoul said with a sinister laugh.

"As if vampires, werewolves, and zombies weren't enough?" Howard replied.

"You might as well stop fighting it. You can't win," Raoul told him in a silky voice. "We've been around forever. We're real, we're here, since the beginning of time. You can't stamp us out." He got up, walking around, warming to his subject. "You persecuted us for being different."

"You're parasites."

"No better or worse than a deadbeat relative or a petty criminal. You're stuck with us, so you better make the best of it."

Howard heard a sound, watching in revulsion as one vampire, then another, detached themselves from the darkness to scurry over to the pools of blood outside their hiding spots. He heard slurping and must have made a face.

"We used to fascinate you."

"That was before I knew what you were."

"What are we?" Raoul bent down to touch his face familiarly. "Monsters?" He shrugged. "We do what we do to survive." He snapped his fingers, and Keisha rose, her eyes blank. She walked toward him. He pulled her down to rest against him, settling her close with an intimacy that made Howard squirm. "You have to get us out of here."

Howard shook his head. "I don't think so."

"You know, I like this one," Raoul said in a friendly manner. "I droned her. Maybe I'll go all the way. Turn her into one of us." He stroked Keisha's face. "Would you like that, my pretty?" he asked softly. He looked at Howard. "You know how we do that, don't you?" The vampire observed the young boy's clenched hands, his gritted teeth. "You wouldn't like that, Howard Drucker," he purred. "You wouldn't like that at all."

Raoul stood easily, taking out a knife from his pocket, freeing Howard's arms. The blood rushed through Howard's abused limbs like needles.

"Oh, I hear it, Raoul. Let me taste it," Sylvie cooed. She rubbed his arms, her tongue flicking with delight. Howard pulled away from her, a sneer on his face.

There was a crash above them. "Come, children," Raoul ordered. "We must flee. Young Howard will lead the way."

He pushed Howard on the shoulder toward the passageway leading to their freedom and Howard's hell.

Chapter 24

Wyatt sprinted toward the part of the park he wanted to go to, and the only area he hadn't seen. He ducked into an empty store, ripped a T-shirt from a hanger and wrapped it around his stinging hand. His hand had stopped bleeding, but he looked like he had just come off a battlefield. He touched his bloody chest with disgust, grabbed another shirt with the theme park logo, and put it on.

In the Monsterland streets there was no light but the dim emergency bulbs that flickered with an orange glow. Merchandise littered the ground, windows gaped, broken, and listless curtains waved like flags of surrender. Wyatt trod carefully, avoiding the dark red puddles. Piles of corpses lay on the pavement. The bodies were unrecognizable.

A barricade separated him from Zombieville. A small suburban town had been built, that much he knew, but it was behind a steel wall, confined in an impenetrable prison, cut off from the rest of the park.

A dismembered body lay on the ground, a steel mesh glove abandoned by its side. A scream split the air, breaking the silence.

The steel gate that held the zombies from society shrieked as a lever groaned, and the gate started its slow movement, opening up Pandora's box. It stopped at the midway point.

Wyatt gingerly picked up the glove, pulling it on his arm. The mesh went all the way to his shoulder, where the leather strap looped over his head to hold it there.

Wyatt heard cries and sporadic shots being fired in the park. The werewolves' triumphant baying made it clear who won the battle. Slowly, the sounds of the violent encounters were dying down.

Overhead, the stars twinkled from the inky sky; even the breeze had died.

Wyatt sucked his breath in, but stopped from inhaling deeply, the sour stench of rotting flesh making the air heavy. He looked back through the alleys and streets he had come down, wishing he could go back, find his brother, and run for safety.

A wolf howled, and he shivered. Jade was somewhere in there. In Zombieville. He had to get her and Nolan out. He put his foot forward and then followed with the other.

He walked toward the metal gate, a solid wall of riveted steel. Wyatt pushed himself to move through it, his eyes searching the darkness.

He reached the attraction, the faint agonizing grunts and muffled moans floating on the still air. He stepped on a porous rock, wincing when the crunch magnified in the dark. A silence followed it, so thick he felt underwater.

Wyatt sniffed, his face grimacing from the stench of decay. It enveloped him, smothering him until he felt his gullet meet the back of his throat. The axe felt heavy in his hands.

He saw them from the corner of his eye. They were slow moving, just like he imagined. They lumbered with a mindless motion, rocking as if their kneecaps didn't work. The zombies were in various stages of the disease, their skin a yellowish green.

Most had their arms outstretched; some had eyes, others empty sockets with sticky black puddles that overflowed to paint their cheekbones in striated patterns.

They shuffled rather than walked, and when the first one moved close enough so that its gnarled fingers brushed against the thick mesh adorning his arm, Wyatt reacted, whacking the axe against its head, watching in sickening astonishment as it cleaved it in two, brains spilling out like water from a broken faucet.

The thing groaned, falling to its knees to land with a soft whisper on the floor. Wyatt backed away, revolted by the rancid stench of the blood, sickened by the way a group fell en masse like a tackle in a football game, the soft sucking and crunching noise of their feast making bile rise so that it coated the back of his throat.

"Jade!" he screamed, his voice cracking. "Jade, where are you?"

Frantic banging answered him from inside one of the houses, and Wyatt raced toward it, mowing down the slow moving zombies in his path.

Chapter 25

Billy leaped by the trash can, a bark forcing him to stop. He turned, spying the new kid. He ran over and licked the cub's ear, which was drenched in blood.

The lad rubbed his face happily against him.

Billy smiled—at first, he had been repulsed by the human when he'd invaded their territory. He was ready to rip his skin, to feast on the warm organs. When he held out the camera, as an offering, Billy's conscience pricked him, and he decided to let him go. The tables turned when the kid begged to be incorporated into the pack.

Little John was horrified. They hadn't added for years—it was a code between them. It was a hard life, but the yearning in those eyes made him do it. A bite, a nip really, and their blood intermingled to morph and change the boy forever.

It was instantaneous, a miracle to watch. The body embraced the changes, the youthful howls shivery in his delight.

Of course, he was sloppy. His initial kill was a messy job, but, Billy thought with pride, *the kid learned fast.* After all, he led them from the confines of the dome to reach the guests enjoying the ride.

"It's eat them or be killed," Billy warned. "No time for maudlin sentimentality like you showed those cops." He gestured to the dead policeman at the base of the mezzanine.

"I don't have a collar like yours," the cub yelped.

"No need. These are collars of captivity. I like yours better," Billy told him with gentle barks. He licked the gold werewolf head pendant. "See, it has green eyes that resemble our lights. You're one of us now."

"For real?" he barked in wonder.

"For real," Billy responded.

Melvin smiled a toothy canine grin and yapped, "Thank you." He then turned to join in the bedlam.

Billy's eyes teared up. "No, thank *you!*" Billy was happy at last. Happy and free, thanks to the boy.

Chapter 26

Carter ran through the miles of halls, trying doors, using his formidable shoulders to break open the locks. He heard sobbing, and he banged on the door, finally kicking it open to find a trio of Monsterland employees huddling in the corner. One rose, brandishing a broom.

"Where is everybody?" Carter demanded.

"Gone. Gone or dead. There's no way out. The wolves have the garage, the zombies just broke through their gate, and the vamps are missing. We're doomed," he cried.

"Have you called for help?"

"We've called Washington. They said help is on the way, but what kind of help?" a girl whined, her face lined with mascara.

"They are going to bomb us; they have to."

Carter agreed grimly. "Where's Vincent?"

The man shrugged. "Probably gone."

Carter shook his head. "He wouldn't leave."

"Try the main control room." He pointed up the dark passageway.

Carter nodded and took off. He heard them close the door, followed by the movement of furniture behind it.

The halls echoed eerily. Carter passed the weapons room, paused, and then ducked inside to grab a shotgun. He stuffed as many shells as he could in his pockets and then loaded the gun. He came up to the control room, trying the doorknob. He double pumped the gun, blasting the locked doorknob so that the door flew open.

Vincent Konrad turned around, his eyes opening wide with surprise. "Officer White, just in time." He held a receiver to his mouth. "No, no, it was nothing. Everything is under control here. The president ... ah yes, the president is in the eating facility, safe and sound. I'm afraid cell phones aren't working well ... I understand. Hmmm ... well, that's no problem." His finger depressed the lever on the base, disconnecting the phone. "The Secretary of State. She's so tiresome. I'll have to do something about her tomorrow."

Carter grabbed the receiver from his hand. He punched in numbers.

"Officer Carter White of the Copper Valley Police Force. We are in trouble here. The president is dead. Security's been breached ..." The line went dead.

Vincent tugged and then held up the phone wire in his fist. "You'll ruin everything. It's all proceeding as it should. I have it all under control. Monsterland is safe."

Carter held up the gun. "You keep saying it's safe, Doctor. Nothing could be further from the truth. It's over, Vincent. Word will get out."

Vincent laughed, flicking on a console. "It already has. It's all over the news." He gestured to the multiple screens in front of him.

The monitors lit up with every news station worldwide reporting on the massacres in all the different Monsterland parks around the world. Thousands were dead—every country had lost leadership. The globe was rudderless. "Right

now, it's just mass confusion. But that won't last." He chuckled. "The new president and I will swoop in." He made a
grandiose movement with his arms. "And save the world."

"I can't even guess how many have died tonight."

"No, you can't. Your simple civil servant brain can't think
larger than Copper Valley." Vincent observed him thought-
fully. "You know what your problem is, White? You have no
vision. You can't see the forest for the trees."

"And you can?" Carter said with contempt.

"Right now, all the governments are reeling. My people
are sliding into planned positions as we speak." He smiled
again, as if reassuring a nervous patient. "Everything is
fixable. Who needed McAdams anyway? He was a liberal with
nasty little ideas. I'm in charge now."

"No, the vice president is in control of the country,"
Carter said slowly as if talking to an idiot.

Vincent threw back his head and laughed. "How do you
think I was introduced to the president? Watch," he said glee-
fully. He pulled out his cell phone. He pressed it so that it was
on speaker.

"Vincent?"

"Nate ... or should I say, President Owens   "

"Is my father safe?"

"He was marvelous. They loved him in the show—tell
him, Carter, tell him how that naughty hunchback stole
the show."

"Hunchback?" Carter asked.

"I've called off the Air Force now that General Anthony is
dead, and the new Chairman of the Joint Chiefs of Staff has
agreed to my wait-and-see approach," the new president
informed him. "I'll deal with the Secretary of State as soon as
I get off the phone with you."

"Excellent, excellent. I couldn't ask for a more perfect
partner." Vincent was all oily charm. He laughed and then
said, "Time to publish the press releases, just as we said." He

glanced at his wristwatch. "By now, every official that attended Monsterland openings in any other part of the world is dead, food for the werewolves. Food for thought, for you, Officer White."

"What are you talking about?" Carter demanded.

"It's simple. For years the Russians have been tampering with our computers, raiding and stealing information. A sort of cyber-terrorism. Well, with the Russians' envoy assassinating the president, as well as every other diplomat attending our parks, it gives President Owens very little choice other than to shut them down. The invasion of Russia's infrastructure starts today. Have you taken down their satellite yet?" He directed the last question to the new president listening on the phone.

"That's crazy; the Russian envoy was murdered," Carter shouted. "They didn't attack."

"Sadly, once word gets out of the massacre here, it won't matter. By then, I will be the new leader of Russia, and I'll add restoring world peace to my resume."

Vincent walked calmly to a console, flicking on screen after screen so that the massacre of Monsterland looked like a cheap horror movie.

"You're mad," Carter whispered. "You're the monster. A monster and murderer."

"No, Officer White. I am brilliant, and I will save the world. I will do what no politicians or diplomats can do—finish the job."

"This was all planned?" Carter asked, with dawning horror.

"A *coup d'état*," Vincent said with a smile, hanging up on the president. He became thoughtful and said, "I used to catch wild pigs when I was a boy. Do you know how to catch wild pigs, Carter?"

"What?" Carter asked.

Vincent studied Carter. He perched his hip casually on one of the desks.

"You catch wild pigs by finding a nice clearing in the woods. You sprinkle corn on the ground. The pigs find it and return every day to eat the food." He folded his hands and then pressed his two index fingers together. He continued. "When they are used to coming every day, you put a fence down one side of the place where they are grazing on the corn. In the beginning, they are wary of the barrier, but eventually, they get used to the fence. They begin to eat the corn again, and you put up another side of the fence. They get used to that and start to eat again. You continue until you have all four sides of the enclosure up with a gate in the last side. Don't you understand?" he asked. "You see, the pigs get used to the free corn and start to come through the gate to eat that corn again. All you have to do is slam the gate on them to catch the whole herd."

He stood, a feverish light in his eyes. "Suddenly the wild pigs have lost their freedom. They run around and around inside the walls, but they are caught. Soon they go back to eating the free corn. They are so used to it that they have forgotten how to forage in the woods for themselves, so they accept their captivity. Monsterland is free corn. We have just captured the entire world." Vincent threw his head back, and the echoes of his laughter bounced off the impregnable wall of his prison. He paused, looked at Carter, and shook his head. "Besides, how else were we to invade Russia? They've been playing with your Internet for years. It's time to have the governments run by more capable hands."

"Monsterland?"

"Oh, my interest in Monsterland was real. We will have theme parks all over the world. It is where we will put trouble-makers. More inventive than prison, don't you think? A zombie police force."

"But the wolves …"

"A means to an end. A careless guard, a lost key, nature takes its course."

"They have the run of the park."

"It appears so … but looks are deceiving."

"But what about the vampires?"

"Nobody cares about them. They are a dying breed. It's the zombies that are valuable. No more expensive prisons. Put malcontents in with the plague victims—again, let nature take its course and poof … problem solved."

"What are you getting for all this?" Carter gestured to the empty room.

"Power. I am the puppeteer. President Owens will follow my directions. You could say we've got a lot in common."

"You're sick," Carter said, disgusted.

"I've been called worse." Vincent sniffed. "Now I think it's time for you to take your place in your new home."

He pressed a button. Carter raised the shotgun.

"I don't think so, Officer White." Vincent drew a small revolver sliding out from his wrist. He shot once, winging Carter, who dropped his shotgun.

Carter recoiled, grabbing his shoulder. Two huge men entered the room. They were wearing uniforms with a new logo that had an American flag on it. It said Federation Forces.

"You thought I was alone," Vincent spat. "I was never alone. You are outnumbered. Long live the new federation!" He punched his fist in the air. "My federation."

"What are you talking about?" Carter's veins bulged as he shouted.

"I have made a worldwide alliance to stop those pesky countries from interfering. Like the Euro and one currency, so shall we all be one nation."

"The single European currency didn't work out so well."

"I'll be the judge of what works and what doesn't succeed, Officer White." A group filed into the room, their faces wooden. "Time to end this."

Carter watched in stupefaction as they took seats.

He heard Vincent order. "Kill the wolves."

One of the men pressed a series of buttons. A high-pitched buzz filled the park. On the screen, the wolves started to run in circles. Their howls penetrated the thick building. The lights on their collars changed from green to red.

"Watch ... watch ... watch," Vincent said eagerly. "We implanted transistors in their collars, only mine have an added kick," he ended on a note of glee.

The earsplitting noise filled the park. The wolves howled, their faces aimed at the moon.

"Here it comes," Vincent said with anticipation, his voice shrill.

One by one, the werewolves rolled and then arced up, their heads exploding in a spectacular eruption. "You're crazy," Carter told him.

"No, genius. Pure genius," Vincent responded. "Give him to the zombies. Wait, I think I want to watch."

Chapter 27

Raoul's hand rested on Howard's shoulder. To someone who didn't know any better, it would appear they were friends. The passageway grew narrower, the sounds from outside louder.

"If we can get past security, there is a way out of here behind the wolf pens." Angie gestured upward and continued. "A drone told me about a feeding pipeline that runs from the back of a supply silo over here."

There was a dark, ominous tower behind the dome of the Werewolf River Run. Angie pointed to a large circular tube that carried food from a special tank toward Zombieville. "It's filled with all kinds of blood and guts," she told them.

Howard swallowed convulsively. He looked at Keisha, trying to make eye contact, but she was as catatonic as the guards.

Screams echoed in the thick air. Raoul's eyes searched the dark streets for signs of the wolves, but he couldn't see any.

"Do you think the wolves got out of the park?" Sylvie asked.

"Doubtful," he replied. "They are too busy gorging themselves on human flesh. Tonight was a smorgasbord for them."

"A Bacchanalian feast." Angie slithered out, drawn to a bright trail of blood on the concrete. She crouched down and wiped her finger through the small puddle. Placing it on her lips, she sucked. "That's vampire blood."

"They didn't stand a chance once the werewolves got out. They are probably all ripped to shreds."

"What?" Howard exclaimed, the old debate supplanting fear in his head. "What of their superior night vision, dexterity, and intelligence?"

"Myths, my little friend. All myths. Just the junk we churned out in our old PR machine to make us more glamorous." Raoul draped his arm around Howard's shoulders in a warm manner. "We are nothing better than vermin that live off the rejects of society." He paused. "Except for me, of course." Raoul considered the supply line. "If we split up—"

"Don't even think about it, Raoul," Ian sneered. He had lost his drones in the melee. "The kid knows his way around. Unless you want to give him to us, and you wake the girl up?"

"Oh, I plan on waking her up," Raoul said with a seductive smile.

Howard felt Sylvie stiffen next to him. She exhaled in a livid huff.

"You think she's prettier than me?" she asked, her eyes watery and hurt. Howard wasn't sure if she was speaking to him or Raoul. The older vampire ignored her with a cold stare. Howard shivered.

Howard looked at Sylvie's deathly pale skin and dirty pink hair. He watched her pat her hair in the age-old feminine way of fussing.

Howard wet his dry lips and considered the most logical way to answer. His brain told him to tell Sylvie that she was more attractive than Keisha. His heart chose this inconvenient time to come to life and twisted painfully when he glanced at Keisha.

Sylvie watched his face, her own turning a dark purple

with rage. Balling her fists, she twirled, punching Keisha full in the chest. Keisha went down like a sack of potatoes, rolling face down on the floor.

There was a tentative howl and a clatter of sharp nails on the empty pavement. Ian craned his neck down the dark alleyways of Monsterland and saw nothing. He moved farther out.

Howard gaped in astonishment, his breath whistling out of him as a massive shape hurtled from the darkness to land with a growl on Ian's chest. They all backed away, watching Ian wrestle with a werewolf, his cries mixed with fierce growls. Ian's teeth gleamed in the moonlight; his sharp nails gripped the wolf by the thick scruff of the neck, trying to twist free.

Angie jumped on its back, and Howard thought, inanely, that it looked like a werewolf sandwich.

Raoul grabbed Keisha's arm and then gripped Howard, pulling them from the tunnel. "Come on, Sylvie!" he ordered.

"You're leaving them?" Howard was aghast.

"I told you I care for nothing," Raoul responded as he herded them toward the supply tube. "Up you go." He pushed Howard onto the riveted bars, forcing him to start climbing onto the winding pipe that disappeared around the other side of the dome.

Howard wrapped his arms around the cold metal tube, wondering, with a shudder, what was coursing through it. The liquid vibrated against his fingertips.

Howard turned in time to see Ian's face being separated from his skull, his dying screams smothered by a spout of blood. The wolf caught Angie around the waist, shaking her limp body like a rag doll.

"Don't look down," Raoul said.

"Too late," Howard wheezed. The wolf stood still, watching him intently. A gold pendant dangled from a chain around its powerful neck, and green glass eyes shined back at him. Howard cocked his head. He knew that pendant.

I guess I was wrong, Howard thought. "Werewolf wins," he said, his voice barely a squeak.

They climbed, their bellies hugging the round metal tube. He heard Keisha cursing loudly as if she were coming back to life. Howard smiled—that was the Keisha he knew.

"What are we doing here?" she complained, her brows lowered.

"Shut up, or I'll drone you again," Raoul warned. He sniffed the air, his face alert. "Zombies."

"This was supposed to take us out of the park," Sylvie moaned. "It took us to the zombies! I'm scared, Raoul. Let's go back."

Raoul kicked out, his face furious, his razor-sharp teeth feral. "Stop whining, you stupid girl." Sylvie grabbed his leg, and they both slipped.

Raoul reached out, taking hold of Howard's ankle, so they all descended in a rush onto the black pavement outside Zombieville. Howard heard Keisha yell, "No!" as his head connected painfully with the concrete. Howard lay flat, staring at the starry sky with a dazed expression.

Keisha leaped down, coming to stand between Howard and Raoul, her stance combative.

"I know taekwondo, you bloodsucking creep."

"You're beautiful when you're angry," Raoul said, walking toward her.

Howard's eyes softened. He wanted to agree. He thought that too.

"Ugh." Keisha gagged. "Is that the best you can do?" She circled him warily, ready to kick.

Howard raised himself, shaking his groggy head. His hand was against something soft, his fingers in a puddle of sticky wetness. He turned over to come face-to-face with the open eyes of a guard, his dead fingers wrapped around the handle of an axe.

Howard reached out to grab the axe, but Raoul walked backward, kicking it out of the way, laughing maniacally.

Raoul growled appreciatively to Keisha, his eyes gleaming. "I'm going to enjoy making a woman out of you." He moved slowly toward her; his eyes dark with passion.

"No," Sylvie screamed, picking up a discarded tree limb, swinging it in a wide arc toward Keisha.

Howard looked around wildly for a weapon. He stood, his hands fisted.

Raoul jumped back, the branch grazing him. He fell, rolling to come up behind Howard, grabbing both his arms in a tight hold, laughing. "I think I like her better, Sylvie. What are you going to do?" He shrugged.

Sylvie bent in half, her mouth opened in a high-pitch scream. Her eyes turned into dark, hot pits of hatred. She moved toward Keisha, using the branch like a javelin.

"Nothing better than a little cat fight," Raoul commented. "We'll flip a coin for the winner. Do you have a quarter?"

Keisha dodged Sylvie with nimble footwork. Sylvie squared off with her, her attention diverted for a minute. They impacted, Keisha's long legs scissoring upward to smash into Sylvie's short form.

Sylvie twisted to come up into a crouch, using the branch to try and trip Keisha. She swiped at the girl's feet, but Keisha jumped high, kicking her in the face.

Raoul winced at the sound of cracking bone. "Ouch, that's got to hurt."

Howard struggled uselessly against Raoul's superior strength. Raising his foot, he brought it down on the vampire's instep. Raoul reacted by punching him in the face. Howard dropped, the lights fading for a minute.

The vampire grabbed him by the lapels, shaking him violently. A sound split the night, and Raoul looked toward the high barrier enclosing Zombieville. It gaped open.

Shuffling feet filled the silent night, followed by the moans of the plague victims. A group of four made their slow way through the half-opened gate toward them. *They walked like, well, zombies.* Howard considered them. They were soft, all squishy—their green skin and stiff, outstretched arms seemed surprisingly fragile.

"One of you better hurry and finish this thing," Raoul called out placidly, his hands still wrapped around Howard's neck. He subdued him. "You could take them," he told Sylvie.

She ignored him, her balled fist connecting with Keisha's chin.

"Stop fighting! *They* are the enemy!" Howard screamed, his stunned look exchanged for sheer horror. He stared at the moving wall of flesh coming their way.

What was wrong with the vamps? Hysteria bubbled in Howard's chest. *They were stronger, more agile; they had superior intelligence; they had working opposable thumbs, for God's sake!* "Move, damn you!" he shouted to Raoul. "Do something!"

Raoul did something then. He placed Howard in front of him to shield him from the approaching zombies.

Howard twisted. Raoul stood behind him, frozen, his eyes wide with ... fear? *Raoul is afraid,* Howard thought disgustedly.

Sylvie fought on with mindless hatred, her sharp nails aiming for Keisha's soft skin.

They were all going to die. Howard had to do something. *Vamps were friggin' useless!* Howard scrambled, feeling his pockets for anything, a key, a pen, a ... pencil.

Howard gripped the pencil in his fist, turning to Raoul's frozen face.

He heard Keisha's cry of dismay as she slid in a slick of blood, going down on one knee. Howard's breath stopped in his throat as he took the number two lead pencil and rammed it directly into Raoul's exposed chest.

"Take this, you bloodsucking leech!" he yelled, his face a frozen grin from the irony that he was driving a wooden stake into the fiend's chest.

He turned to see Keisha's prone body roll to the side, reaching out to grab the discarded axe a few feet from the body of the dead guard.

Howard yelled, "Keisha! Use the wooden handle!"

Keisha looked at the axe head and then at the handle. She slammed the axe on the concrete, separating the metal and leaving a sharp splintered point.

With a war cry, she ran straight for Sylvie, impaling the vampire straight through the heart. Sylvie dropped where she stood, her skin turning mottled as blood rushed from her mouth in a dying breath.

Keisha was panting, and she fell to her knees. Howard raced over, propping her arm over his shoulder.

"I think I love you," said Howard. He grabbed her, kissing her fully and passionately on the lips. Keisha's opened eyes drifted shut.

Keisha pulled away to study him. "Now you get romantic?"

The sound of moaning interrupted them. She glanced behind her, watching as the zombies landed on Raoul's body, their satisfied mouths chomping on his limbs. "Ugh."

"Let's get out of here."

They turned to flee—a werewolf stood, growling, blocking their exit. It was tense, its muscles bulging under fur, twin green chips of glass reflecting against the pelt. Howard considered the beast's intelligent hazel eyes, and his mouth dropped open.

Keisha tugged his arm, her knees weakening in fear.

Spinning, they saw the zombies look up, their faces cocked with interest, their lifeless eyes deep pockets of emptiness.

Keisha yanked her broken axe handle from Sylvie's body, brandishing it, while Howard took out another number two pencil from his pocket protector.

The lone wolf howled from behind them.

"Crap," Howard muttered.

Chapter 28

Wyatt scrambled through the streets, the axe in front of him, his mesh-covered arm outstretched. Bushes parted, and two men came at him—one was on his knees, which were now bloody stumps, and the other was in a lesser state of decay.

Wyatt swung the axe. It connected with the soft middle of the taller man. Wyatt jumped back, avoiding the blood and bone that flew out. The corpse fell to the artificial turf with a dull thud.

The man on his knees made a grunting sound like a rooting pig. He knocked the axe from Wyatt's hand. Wyatt reached out with his meshed arm, the fingers sinking into the eye sockets, and he pulled hard. The head came off with a soft *whish*, the grinding sound of the gristle and bone making Wyatt gag.

He spun in a circle, throwing the disconnected head at another group of shuffling zombies that fell like bowling pins. "Strike," Wyatt said with satisfaction. He paused, realizing with a start that they were incredibly fragile.

Bending, he picked up the heavy axe and ran through the

devastation into the house where he heard a steady thrum of knocking.

Dust motes danced in the air, the waning moonlight illuminating them like fairy dust. The sky had lightened somewhat, and Wyatt wondered what time it was.

He searched the gloom. A woman lay on the floor, dragging herself toward him. She moaned piteously.

Wyatt screamed Jade's name, ducking into the dark corners, his feet shoving the slow-moving wrecks of humanity that crawled along the floor. They grabbed at his legs, squeezing his thighs.

Using his axe handle, he butted them away, watching in revulsion as body parts broke off to land with muffled thumps on the floor. He picked off their relentless hands, chopping with the ease of a butter knife, their diseased limbs falling in a cascade of carnage.

He kicked the slow-moving woman out of the way, yanking open the door to a bedroom, finding Jade cowering in a corner. Wyatt rested the axe against the wall and peeled off the bloody mesh armor from his arm.

He pulled her into his embrace, and she curled up against him, her body shaking with dry-heaving sobs.

"It's okay. I've got you. What happened to your protective gear?"

"Once we heard the alarms, we tried to run. It was too heavy, and Nolan made me take it off."

"Where's Nolan?" Wyatt asked.

"Nolan …" she stuttered between gulps. "Nolan …"

"Did he leave you here alone?" Wyatt cupped her face with his hands.

Jade's blue eyes widened until the irises were fully surrounded by white. Her mouth opened in a soundless scream.

"What?" he demanded.

Jade peeked over his shoulder fearfully.

Wyatt placed himself in front of Jade protectively. Nolan was behind him, his eyes filled with an unholy light, his skin a sickly shade of green in the dark room.

"Nolan, man. You scared me …" Wyatt said, turning back to Jade.

"Wyyyatt!" Jade jumped, grabbing at his shoulders. She pointed at Nolan, who grinned evilly. Wyatt sniffed and then peered closer in the gloom.

Nolan appeared … strange. He smelled foul. A large chunk of skin was missing from his forearm. Nolan's eyes had sunk into his skull, and he held his arms outstretched, ready to wrap his hands around Wyatt's throat. His voice was as dry as a hacksaw, but it still worked.

"I knew you wanted her, you creep." Nolan clenched his hands, and the skin on them looked waterlogged, as though he had been underwater for hours.

Wyatt's hair stood up on his scalp when he noticed the telltale white spots on Nolan's bluish nails.

"What happened to you?"

"Nothin'." Nolan grinned in a parody of a smile. "Come on, buddy; I'm *desperate* to have a word with you."

Wyatt backed near a closet, feeling Jade behind him. They were trapped in the room; there was no escape.

"Can't we talk about this?"

Nolan laughed, a raw, scraped sound. "You think I'm just going to let you have her? She locked herself away from me a long time ago. She told me this was our last date, didn't you, Jade?" He leered behind Wyatt. "You think I didn't see her making eyes at you for the last few weeks? Did you?" He tapped Wyatt hard on the chest. Wyatt pushed him away. Skin sloughed off to hang like a drape on Nolan's wrist.

Wyatt stared at the bloody hands, sucking in his stomach to avoid a second touch.

"Well, babe, you were right about one thing. This will be

our last date, and it's going to last a long, long time," Nolan told Jade.

She wailed.

"Shh …" Wyatt warned her. "You'll bring more of them in here." He pushed her further behind him, but Jade moved in front of him defiantly.

"I hate you, Nolan. You're a bully." Jade stood rigidly in front of Wyatt. "I never liked you, but I was afraid to not go out with you." She turned to Wyatt. "He made me date him. I hate him."

Nolan bent his diseased face close to Jade, looming over her. "Be afraid, Jade," Nolan spat. "Be really afraid. Remember when I twisted your arm. Remember how it felt?"

Jade spit viciously in his face, a glob of saliva landing on the putty skin of his cheek.

Nolan reacted impulsively, shoving her hard so that she hit the wall with a loud crash and slumped to the floor.

Wyatt felt his chest tighten; his face grew red. He balled his fists impotently, because to touch Nolan, he risked infection. Nolan reached out to Wyatt, and he dodged his arm, easily.

"Yeah. Stupid little Jade. I told her I'd beat the crap out of her little brother if she didn't go out with me," Nolan snickered.

Nolan moved closer, almost on top of him. His hand was inches from Wyatt's unprotected neck. Wyatt closed his eyes in resignation, knowing he was doomed. He looked up to stare death in the face.

"Hey, Nolan," Wyatt heard Jade's voice from behind.

Nolan craned around almost dislocating his neck.

"I'm breaking up with you."

The axe hung suspended as if in midair. It wasn't until Nolan's body was split in two that Wyatt watched in astonishment as Jade triumphantly pulled the axe out of Nolan's lifeless back.

Nolan collapsed like an empty suit of clothes.

Wyatt grabbed her hand and said, "Let's get out of here." He took the axe from Jade.

They bolted from the room to find zombies crowding against the windows outside, blocking what little light could come in. Wyatt cracked the door, then slammed it shut. They were outnumbered, and there was no way out.

Jade turned to him and said, "How are we going to get out of here?"

Wyatt looked at her and replied, "I'm going to rush them and make a path for you."

As soon as the words left his mouth, they heard the thud of zombies dropping like flies outside.

Wyatt peeked out the window to see a lone zombie methodically smashing the heads of the plague victims. He was using a small boulder to do the deed.

Was he eliminating competition or creating an escape route?

Wyatt's eyes met the creature's, and he knew instinctively, the thing meant them no harm. Wyatt opened the door.

"Out," the zombie rasped painfully. "Out, get out of here." The zombie dropped the boulder and grabbed his throat from the pain of speaking.

Wyatt didn't need any more encouragement than that. Grabbing Jade's hand, the axe in the other, he turned sideways. Stopping for a second, he said, "Thanks."

The zombie seemed exhausted by the effort. Raising his hand, he pointed to the gateway, whispering, "Now."

Wyatt dashed from the door, dragging Jade behind him. More zombies came at them like a driving rain, but Wyatt was fast, dodging through them as if they were a sloppy defensive line, swinging his axe like a claymore.

The muted light beckoned from the gate, and the sky lightened. Wyatt's feet tore up the grass, and he heard Jade panting behind him, but he held her in a merciless grip.

Bowing his head with determination, he pressed on, his heart pumping like a steam engine, the gate his only goal.

He reached the metal barrier, swinging Jade through, turning to see that strange male zombie shoving his pursuers onto the ground and then crushing their legs so they couldn't follow.

Chapter 29

Wyatt rounded the gate and then pulled it on the wheels to close it, but he couldn't move it far enough alone. It was too heavy. He heard Jade's intake of breath, and, when he turned, he saw a werewolf standing, blocking off the main exit. His name was being called, and to his left were Keisha and a bloody-looking Howard Drucker, holding her hand.

Wyatt glanced to each of them, the breath leaving his body at the relief of seeing his friends. Between them were the torn and bloodied carcasses of a dozen zombies.

Howard Drucker looked at Wyatt and then the wolf and back to Keisha.

"I feel like I'm stuck in *The Good, the Bad and the Ugly*," Howard shouted.

"Well, I'm not gonna be ugly," Keisha retorted. "So that leaves good and bad."

Howard gazed at Keisha with a dopey grin. "I think we're bad. Super bad."

Keisha smiled. "Okay, genius, how are we going to get out of this one? I don't think your number two pencil is going to work on him." She gestured to the wolf with a nod of her head.

Howard looked at the spot. The wolf was gone.

Wyatt ran to Howard and Keisha. "You guys okay?" He grabbed Howard by both upper arms.

Howard held up his bloody pencil. "Never better. Where's Nolan?"

"Nolan split," Wyatt said.

"You wouldn't believe it," Howard told him. "We were about to be annihilated by a group of zombies, and some wolf tore them to shreds."

"Where is it?" Wyatt searched.

"It disappeared."

Headlights lit up the road. A golf cart filled with four men pulled into the clearing. Behind the cart, the sun peeked its way over the rocky hills. The sky lightened to a lilac hue.

"Ah, Alec Baldwin," Vincent Konrad said as he stepped out of the cart.

"Wyatt," he corrected him. He watched Carter being pulled from the back of the vehicle. His shirt was torn, and his shoulder was bloody. His face hadn't fared too well either. A man bashed him on his bad shoulder with a shotgun. Carter groaned, then fell to his knees. Another hopped out of the cart, kicking him in the stomach.

Wyatt surged forward but found himself imprisoned by the iron grip of one of Vincent's henchmen. He looked around. They were surrounded by a ring of guards in uniforms he hadn't seen before. They were all armed with rifles.

"Carter!"

"A family reunion. Eh, Frank? What do you think of your boy?" Vincent called to the lone zombie, who staggered from the small space where he had squeezed through the gate.

"Wyatt," Vincent directed a question to him, his face filled with mirth. "What do you call a lawyer who turns into a zombie?"

Wyatt looked at Vincent and then at the wreck of a man who stood on unsteady legs. "What ... are you ... doing?" The words were wrenched from the zombie's throat. "This was ... supposed ... to be ... a place of learning ... and science."

Vincent went on as if he hadn't heard him. "You didn't answer my riddle. What do you call a lawyer who turns into a zombie? Don't know? I'll tell you. Frank Baldwin. No relation to Alec, of course." Vincent laughed at his joke. "To Alec, get it?"

Wyatt sagged against the guard and then his face inched up to come to land on the shell of humanity that stood swaying in the center. "It can't be." Wyatt's heart sank. "It looks nothing like my father!" Wyatt shouted, tears streaming down his face.

Vincent came forward like a demented game show host. "It can be, and it is. Oh, how I wish I had the press here, but, sadly, they are all dead. No more press but mine from now on. Thank you very much."

There was a scuffle, and a group of zombies broke free from the gate to make their slow way toward them. Vincent nodded, and two guards moved forward, spraying them with bullets. They dropped where they stood.

Carter was shoved against Wyatt. He tottered, and Wyatt held out a hand to steady him. He sank to his knees and then leaned against Wyatt's leg, his face down.

"Do you know what's going on?" Wyatt asked.

Carter shook his head. He had a cut over his eye, and his cheek was bruised.

"Do you?" Wyatt asked again. He looked at his birth father, searching for something recognizable, but found nothing.

Carter's eyes found Wyatt. "I didn't know about that. I know your dad—"

"Worked for me, Wyatt. He was my attorney. Your mother

was not happy with that. Said he worked too hard, ignored the family. Felt the work was unethical. Imagine that, an unethical lawyer. An oxymoron, if I ever heard one. You know," Vincent confided, "I helped with the arrangements in the divorce. Used a crack LA team that knows the ins and outs of hiding funds from pesky families. They hadn't been getting along for a while, right, Frank?" Vincent supplied helpfully. "I couldn't have my attorney distracted. He had work to do. Besides, he believed in me. Believed with so much passion that he left all his money to my research." He turned to Frank. "You weren't supposed to get infected, you stupid man. I told you to keep your hands to yourself. Never could keep his hands off the ladies." Vincent shrugged. "*C'est la vie.* Now he'll have his son with him for as long as he lasts."

The zombie raised a hand—his destroyed vocal chords grunted, but the sounds were little more than groans. His mouth shaped the word *no.* His sad eyes looked from Carter to Wyatt. He pointed to Vincent, his face changing into a sneer. He moved toward the doctor, anger written all over his face.

Vincent backed away. "Now, now, Frank. What's all this? Suddenly you care about the boy. You and I both know you didn't give a damn about anything except for money." Vincent's laugh was cut short when the zombie picked up speed in a burst of energy. Vincent's eyes opened wide with fear, and he screamed, "Shoot him. Shoot him now!"

A shot rang out, and Frank Baldwin fell to his knees. He wobbled for a second, then collapsed. His eyes locking with Wyatt's before they closed forever.

Wyatt turned and grabbed the axe that lay behind him. Carter pulled himself up and then moved in front of Wyatt, knocking him to the ground as another shot rang out. Wyatt felt Carter fall against him and cried out, "Dad!" taking Carter into his arms.

Vincent turned to the guard. "Finish them off." He walked toward the cart, dismissing them.

The guard raised his rifle. A long black shadow raced from between two buildings, ripping off his arm, and the shot went wide. The wolf grabbed the gun and then turned, laying it at Wyatt's feet. A gold pendant with green glass eyes filled Wyatt's vision. The wolf panted and then spun, leaping to attack the throat of another guard.

"Look, werewolves!" Howard pointed to the west, distracting them. Everyone turned to look in that direction.

Wyatt picked up the gun, but the remaining soldiers broke rank, disappearing into the rubble.

Vincent turned, his voice panicked. "Stop, you imbeciles. You're supposed to protect me! I'm the leader of your world."

Vincent jumped into his cart, turning abruptly to make his escape. Wyatt held up the rifle, and all things around him turned soft—the only thing he could focus on was the round shape of Vincent's dark head. He felt a tug on his leg. Carter looked up, his face bleached white but his voice firm. "Close one eye, and aim for the biggest part of him, son."

Wyatt nodded, relief filling his chest. "You okay?"

"Flesh wound. Just shoot the son of a bitch."

The gun fit against his shoulder as if he had held it a hundred times. He didn't think about the sound. His world shrank to his father's corpse, the reassuring weight of Carter against his leg, and the outline of Vincent's head. Closing one eye, he squeezed the trigger. Nothing happened. He clicked it open—the chamber was empty.

He heard Carter's soft curse as he hauled himself to his feet.

The wolf circled, leaping over a cluster of dead bodies, its long body stretching over the road, almost airborne. The five of them saw the cart roll over from the impact of the wolf hitting it. Vincent tumbled down the soft side of the road and then scrambled to his feet to escape down the path.

The wolf easily ran after him, leaping on his back so that he fell clumsily. He reached into his pocket to aim a small gun, but the wolf stretched out with his snout, clamping his jaw on Vincent's wrist, pulling. Vincent watched in revolted fascination as his hand detached. He screamed, high and long, the sound echoing in the empty park.

The wolf jumped on his chest—the sound was cut short. Vincent rolled, sobbing for the wolf to leave him be. The animal allowed him to crawl away. He scrabbled on the ground to escape. Vincent looked back, relief flooding his face. "Thank you," he cried. "Thank you. I will take care of you. I will reward you."

He rambled on; his voice was desperate. The wolf raised its head to give a long howl. Everything stopped, even Vincent, who turned to look back. He must have seen something the others didn't, because he raised his bloody stump, screaming, "Noooooooooooooo—" The wolf raced to him, the shriek died as the werewolf tore Vincent's head off in a single yank.

The werewolf trotted away, its prize between its long fangs, Vincent's lifeless eyes staring back at them, mouth caught in a soundless scream. The wolf shook the head, then flung it into the bowels of the theme park.

"Melvin was right all along," Wyatt said with admiration.

Keisha turned to Howard and said, "I told you, Howard Drucker, vamps are useless."

"Dang it!" Howard responded, with a grin.

They watched quietly as the last werewolf took a flying leap over the concrete wall to disappear into the shimmering desert.

"Let's get out of here," Wyatt said, taking Jade's hand in his own.

Carter nodded as he limped over to the dead guard to pick up a gun. He searched the sky, noticing the sun painting the ridge of the eastern mountains.

"First we have to lock the zombies in." They followed him to the barricade. They all worked together to shove the iron gate closed. There was a muted fumble on the other side followed by the soft thud of the zombies impacting the hard surface.

The iron clanked loudly as the lock slid into place.

Overhead, a trio of Air Force jets zoomed low, made a wide curving arc, and flew over again. In the distance, a sea of black helicopters flooded the sky, heading with determination toward the park.

"I guess the military has decided to reassert themselves," Carter said.

"What?" Wyatt asked.

Howard walked next to him, placing his fingers over his eyes to shade them from the slowly rising sun. "It means our government has gone back to work."

"Sean?" Carter questioned, turning to Wyatt.

Wyatt checked his phone, reading messages, his eyes tearing up. "Home, safe with Mom. She's freaking out. I have forty-five messages from her. Should I tell her we're okay?"

Carter hooked his arm around Wyatt's neck.

"Yep. We're okay."

In the rusty-orange-colored hills, the sun rose, coating them with warmth, and a lone wolf howled.

Acknowledgments

Monsterland always resided within me from the first time I stepped into a theme park as a kid. While I enjoyed conventional rides with both anticipation and fear, I never understood why there wasn't a more primal theme park created, one that captured what scares us most—monsters. *Monsterland* was born on a lazy summer afternoon, after a classic-movies marathon binge. The story took shape and became so much more than a fear of monsters, but that of a group of teens teetering on the cusp of adulthood, and as the story grew, so many current issues from bullying to finding acceptance and happiness in one's own skin, found their way into the manuscript. This is so much more than a monster book, and I hope the readers see that. I couldn't have written *Monsterland* without the love and support, as well as the professionalism and expertise of the following people:

Sharon—you have been, and remain, a source of serenity and patience. Your hand is the only one I want to hold on the Werewolf River Run.

Mom—you are the voice of reason. You have always taught me "To thine own self be true." This book would not exist if not for your guidance and foresight. And for the funding of my expedition as well. Big thanks for that.

Dad—thank you for being my rock. Also, please don't read or listen to this book. I don't want to be called any colorful names.

Eric—thank you making me put in the werewolves and vampires. You are my drummer in the band of life, keeping a steady beat to this crazy thing that's happening to us.

Jennifer—thank you for keeping me grounded by constantly hitting me over the head. I'm grateful for that.

Alexander & Cayla—you are the reason why I'm doing this.

Hallie & Zachary—you are also the reason why I'm doing this.

Susan—it took me 28 years to find you. But as you said on our first call "It was kismet." I'm really looking forward to the next 28.

Nick—thank you for being my rock star agent. You took a chance on me, and for that, I will be forever grateful. I still think it was the bacon cheeseburgers we had at that amazing restaurant in Brooklyn, though.

Kim—you were on my vision board for years. Thank you for seeing through the monsters and into the heart of Monsterland. This is just the first step in our journey together.

Kevin you have taught me more in one year than I learned in 11 years of English classes. Thank you for opening the park.

The production team at WordFire Press—I couldn't have asked for a more professional job on the manuscript. I promise I'm done with the changes. No really, I am.

Julie & Brittney—my sincerest gratitude for putting *Monsterland* on the map.

And to all the readers out there—your comments and support have made everything worthwhile. Thank you all.

About the Author

Michael Okon is an award-winning and best-selling author of multiple genres, including paranormal, thriller, horror, action/adventure and self-help. He graduated from Long Island University with a degree in English, and then later received his MBA in business and finance. Coming from a family of writers, he has storytelling is his DNA. Michael has been writing from as far back as he can remember, his inspiration being his love for films and their impact on his life. From the time he saw *The Goonies*, he was hooked on the idea of entertaining people through unforgettable characters.

Michael is a lifelong movie buff, a music playlist aficionado, and a sucker for self-help books. He lives on the North Shore of Long Island with his wife and children.

Monsterland 2 is coming soon.

Web: www.michaelokon.com

Twitter: @IAmMichaelOkon

Facebook: IAmMichaelOkon

If You Liked

Death Warmed Over by Kevin J. Anderson
Unnatural Acts by Kevin J. Anderson
Working Stiff by Kevin J. Anderson
The Love-Haight Case Files by Jean Rabe & Donald J. Bingle